WYATT'S MISSION

BROTHERHOOD PROTECTORS WORLD

TEAM EAGLE
BOOK FIVE

JEN TALTY

Copyright © 2023, Jen Talty

This book is a work of fiction. Names, characters, places and incidents are products of the author's imagination or used fictitiously. Any resemblance to actual events, locales or persons living or dead is entirely coincidental.

© 2023 Twisted Page Press, LLC ALL RIGHTS RESERVED

No part of this book may be used, stored, reproduced or transmitted without written permission from the publisher except for brief quotations for review purposes as permitted by law.

This book is licensed for your personal enjoyment only. This book may not be re-sold or given away to other people. If you would like to share this book with another person, please purchase an additional copy for each recipient. If you're reading this book and did not purchase it, or it was not purchased for your use only, please purchase your own copy.

PRAISE FOR JEN TALTY

"Deadly Secrets is the best of romance and suspense in one hot read!" *NYT Bestselling Author Jennifer Probst*

"A charming setting and a steamy couple heat up the pages in a suspenseful story I couldn't put down!" *NY Times and USA today Bestselling Author Donna Grant*

"Jen Talty's books will grab your attention and pull you into a world of relatable characters, strong personalities, humor, and believable storylines. You'll laugh, you'll cry, and you'll rush to get the next book she releases!" Natalie Ann USA Today Bestselling Author

"I positively loved *In Two Weeks*, and highly recommend it. The writing is wonderful, the story is fantastic, and the characters will keep you coming back for more. I can't wait to get my hands on future installments of the NYS Troopers series." *Long and Short Reviews*

"*In Two Weeks* hooks the reader from page one. This is a fast paced story where the development of the romance grabs you emotionally and the suspense keeps you sitting on the edge of your chair. Great characters, great writing, and a believable plot that can be a warning to all of us." *Desiree Holt, USA Today Bestseller*

"*Dark Water* delivers an engaging portrait of wounded hearts as the memorable characters take you on a healing journey of love. A mysterious death brings danger and intrigue into the drama, while sultry passions brew into a believable plot that melts the reader's heart. Jen Talty pens an entertaining romance that grips the heart as the colorful and dangerous story unfolds into a chilling ending." *Night Owl Reviews*

"This is not the typical love story, nor is it the typical mystery. The characters are well rounded and interesting." *You Gotta Read Reviews*

"*Murder in Paradise Bay* is a fast-paced romantic thriller with plenty of twists and turns to keep you guessing until the end. You won't want to miss this one..." *USA Today best-selling author Janice Maynard*

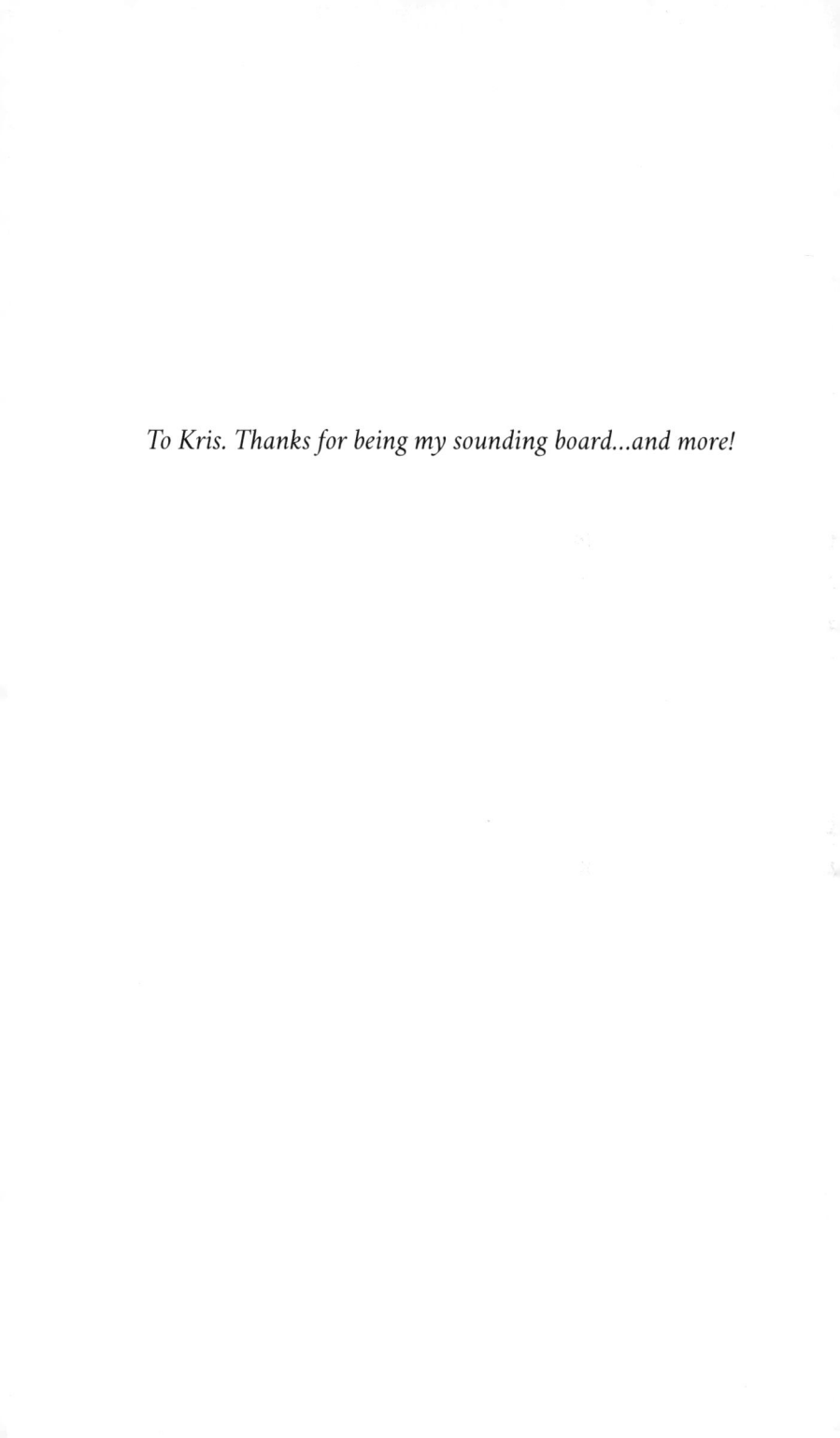

To Kris. Thanks for being my sounding board...and more!

BROTHERHOOD PROTECTORS
ORIGINAL SERIES BY ELLE JAMES

Brotherhood Protectors Series
Montana SEAL (#1)
Bride Protector SEAL (#2)
Montana D-Force (#3)
Cowboy D-Force (#4)
Montana Ranger (#5)
Montana Dog Soldier (#6)
Montana SEAL Daddy (#7)
Montana Ranger's Wedding Vow (#8)
Montana SEAL Undercover Daddy (#9)
Cape Cod SEAL Rescue (#10)
Montana SEAL Friendly Fire (#11)
Montana SEAL's Mail-Order Bride (#12)
SEAL Justice (#13)
Ranger Creed (#14)
Delta Force Rescue (#15)
Dog Days of Christmas (#16)
Montana Rescue (#17)
Montana Ranger Returns (#18)

BROTHERHOOD PROTECTORS
WORLD

ORIGINAL SERIES BY ELLE JAMES

Brotherhood Protectors Colorado World
Team EAGLE
Booker's Mission - Kris Norris
Hunter's Mission - Kendall Talbot
Gunn's Mission - Delilah Devlin
Xavier's Mission - Lori Matthews
Wyatt's Mission - Jen Talty

Team Raptor
Darius' Promise - Jen Talty
Simon's Promise - Leanne Tyler
Nash's Promise - Stacey Wilk
Spencer's Promise - Deanna L. Rowley
Logan's Promise - Kris Norris

Team Falco
Fighting for Esme - Jen Talty
Fighting for Charli - Leanne Tyler
Fighting for Tessa - Stacey Wilk
Fighting for Kora - Deanna L. Rowley
Fighting for Fiona - Kris Norris

Athena Project
Beck's Six - Desiree Holt

Victoria's Six - Delilah Devlin
Cygny's Six - Reina Torres
Fay's Six - Jen Talty
Melody's Six - Regan Black

Team Trojan
Defending Sophie - Desiree Holt
Defending Evangeline - Delilah Devlin
Defending Casey - Reina Torres
Defending Sparrow - Jen Talty
Defending Avery - Regan Black

Brotherhood Protectors Yellowstone World
Team Wolf
Guarding Harper - Desiree Holt
Guarding Hannah - Delilah Devlin
Guarding Eris - Reina Torres
Guarding Payton - Jen Talty
Guarding Leah - Regan Black

Brotherhood Protectors Yellowstone World
Team Eagle
Booker's Mission - Kris Norris
Hunter's Mission - Kendall Talbot
Gunn's Mission - Delilah Devlin
Xavier's Mission - Lori Matthews
Wyatt's Mission - Jen Talty

CHAPTER 1

Wyatt Bixby carefully removed his headset. He didn't want to disturb the delicate balance he'd managed to maintain in his brain while he teetered on the brink of death. He jumped from the helicopter. "Shit." He forgot to put his weight on his left knee. He hobbled toward the hangar, groaning with every step.

"When will you remember you're not twenty anymore and you have a bum leg?" Booker asked.

"The same day you stop skimming the tops of trees and piloting that thing like you're trying to impress a lady. You got the girl and for some strange fucking reason, I'm still your best friend."

"At least I don't drive like a crop duster." Booker laughed, pointing to Xavier who strolled across the tarmac with Gunnar. "Have you ever been up in a small plane with Xavier? Hand to God, I thought he would crash into the cornfield last time I went up with him. He pulls up high and dives straight down. Even I was hanging on to the holy shit bar for a second."

"Not sure I've seen corn in these parts, but if I do, I'll remember to cue the music that matches the movie." Wyatt paused at the door of the hangar to rub his knee. When he bent over, a wave of nausea filled his head. Fuck. That was the last thing he needed. The injuries he suffered from the crash that had taken away his career as a Navy SEAL weren't overly bothersome until they were.

And then they were fucking debilitating.

The dislocated knee had caused some arthritis and acted up when he pushed too hard or landed on it wrong. It might not have ended his career if he weren't pushing forty.

But the migraines and what the doctors called post-traumatic vertigo from a brain injury certainly did, especially since it had been a year and a half since the crash and symptoms still plagued him. It didn't happen very often and both his memory and concentration had improved by leaps and bounds, but these occasional bouts made him batshit crazy.

"I need water," Booker said. "I'll get you some too."

"That would be great." Wyatt made his way inside, finding a chair. The nausea usually hit him first, then the stars, and then the headache. When it was bad, all

Wyatt could do was find a dark room, a bed, and sleep it off.

Booker knew better than to bring attention to what was happening. It had been eight months since Wyatt had gotten a migraine that put him down. The medication he'd been taking to ward them off had been working, but the doctor warned them there could be triggers.

Certain foods.

Stress.

Bright lights.

Or sudden movements, like the jerky ones a helicopter made while avoiding trees. But if Wyatt was going to be able to stay employed with the Aviation Division of the Brotherhood Protectors, his body needed to handle the flying that Booker had just put him through.

"Here you go." Booker handed him a water bottle.

Wyatt reached into his pocket and pulled out the tiny packet he'd forced himself to carry wherever he went. Carefully, he opened it and took out the pill. He hated taking it. The idea made him feel as though he was weak. He knew that was as ridiculous as Booker feeling responsible for the crash that ended their careers and killed good men. He popped one of the pills and swallowed.

He was required to document the headache with the Brotherhood Protectors medical staff. Glancing at his watch, he noted the time of onset. The pain registered at four out of ten. Mild and within the limit he needed to be employed. The queasy stomach didn't make him want to rush to the bathroom and the stars had already left him. But his vision had become slightly blurry and his body felt like he was on the water, not land.

Booker pulled up a chair, flipped it, and then straddled it. He munched on a bag of chips, offering Wyatt some, knowing food often helped.

"No, thanks," Wyatt said, thankful his friend didn't ask all the dumb questions about how he was feeling.

Migraines sucked and Wyatt feared they could end his career with the Brotherhood Protectors. If he got one worse than this while on a mission and it couldn't be managed by medication, there was no way he could do his job effectively.

He sucked in a deep breath and held it for ten seconds before letting it out slowly. Staring at Booker's dirty boots, he focused on the shoelaces. It helped to remain steady while he gave the medication a chance to kick in. He was lucky that not only did his system respond quickly to the drug, but it worked. He'd read that it didn't for many. He also took another medication once a day to help ward off the migraines. That one had taken a while to get used to because it increased his brain fog, which at the time was pretty bad from the head injury he'd suffered.

Now, he didn't notice it at all or have much

problem with concentration. Well, not any more than he did before the crash. He'd always had a slight issue with being easily distracted. It drove his parents crazy when he'd been a kid. The military had forced him to learn patience and had given him the ability to focus.

Right now, he needed something very different.

"How goes things with you and Callie?" Wyatt asked. "I can't imagine living with a woman."

"It's not anything like you'd think. And Callie's amazing. It's been an adjustment, but it's cool." Booker winked. "And she's a much better kisser than you." Booker and Wyatt had been friends for what seemed like forever. There wasn't anyone who knew Wyatt better and vice versa. Wyatt knew how much in love his buddy was with Callie. How perfect they were for each other and that living together had been an easy step. Wyatt had been to their place for dinner. He'd become close with Callie and people around the Brotherhood Protectors Aviation Division called them the three musketeers.

Wyatt didn't mind. He appreciated Callie and she never tried to change Booker and while the time Wyatt and Booker spent together was less, Callie always encouraged a boys' night. She never interfered in what everyone referred to as a bromance.

Wyatt lifted a finger and waggled it. "You didn't get the full Wyatt experience and you never will. You're not deserving of it." He shifted his gaze, checking to see if the room went with him or followed his gaze a second or two later.

He let out a sigh of relief. The medication was doing what it was supposed to. He sat up taller and rounded his shoulders, doing a full assessment.

Pain at a three.

Nausea nearly gone. That was excellent.

No stars.

He turned his head left. Then right. There was maybe half a second delay, but it didn't make him feel sick or increase the pressure between his temples.

Another ten minutes and he'd be fine.

Thank fucking God.

"Ouch. That hurt, man." Booker tapped his chest. "Is Kirby still coming? Callie is looking forward to getting to know her better." Booker arched a brow. This was the only topic that Wyatt had been trying to avoid for weeks. The last time he'd seen Kirby had been five months ago. She'd come home for her parents' fortieth wedding anniversary and made a special trip to West Yellowstone to visit Wyatt. She stayed a few days and then was gone, which was typical Kirby.

She cared more about her gorillas than she did humans and Wyatt understood why.

Her passion for her work drew Wyatt to Kirby. He understood her drive and commitment because he'd had it as a Navy SEAL and now with the Aviation Division of the Brotherhood Protectors. That always made him laugh because flying wasn't something he enjoyed and the only person he wanted to go up in the air with was Booker. Well, he'd do it with Xavier. He was a skilled pilot. He trusted him with his life. However, Wyatt couldn't control the fear factor with anyone in the captain's seat other than Booker. That was a reality that he had never been able to shake no matter how hard he tried. It had nothing to do with anyone's ability and everything to do with a single childhood trauma that left an imprint on Wyatt's psyche that could never be changed.

Wyatt got a lot of shit for that, especially from Xavier and Hunter. He loved those two like brothers. They'd done a few joint missions together over the years. They were in the same career-ending crash. They all went through rehab together and ended up with the Brotherhood Protectors as Team Eagle. They were good men. The best.

Of course, they all told Wyatt he was being ridiculous and their flying was perfection. Wyatt honestly couldn't argue, but that didn't make his fears vanish.

"Last I heard she landed Stateside last night," Wyatt said. "She needed to check on the supplies. If all went well, she should be in the air now, landing at eight." He pulled out his phone. "At least according to her messages."

"You haven't spoken to her?"

"Only texts," Wyatt said.

Once Kirby returned to the Congo and became immersed with the gorillas and her work, she didn't make phone calls. She did message him occasionally, and sometimes those conversations lasted an hour or more. They chatted about work or family, and a time or two it turned sexual.

He always enjoyed those conversations.

But it was rarely serious. They weren't in a relationship. They were friends who had sex.

And Kirby made sure he knew it.

Wyatt glanced at his cell. "Shit. There was a problem with her supplies and now she's delayed and will have to take a later flight." Her time in the States was always short-lived. A week to ten days at the most, if he was lucky. The last time she was here, he only got to see her for a few nights because she had to spend it with her family, whom she avoided as much as she could.

That shouldn't annoy him, but it did. Especially since he'd faced the fact that he did love her and had been in love with her for years.

Hell, she'd been the only woman he'd been with for the last five years except for two fleeting relationships he'd tried because he didn't want to admit Kirby was the one woman who fit in his life.

"What kind of issue?" Booker asked.

"She didn't say." Wyatt quickly shot Kirby a text back letting her know he'd be able to pick her up no matter the time. "Nor does she know when she'll be arriving."

Xavier, Gunn, and Hunter strolled across the hangar in his direction. Wyatt did another quick check of his symptoms, making sure his brain had accepted the meds. He rated the migraine as a two. That was at least functional. He rolled his neck and glanced left and right.

There was no lag in his vision.

Progress.

"We're headed to the pub for a beer," Xavier said with a big fat grin. "Men only. You two coming?"

"I'm in. Just let me call Callie and tell her what's up." Booker jumped to his feet.

Sometimes it sucked being the only single guy. Since arriving in West Yellowstone, everyone on Team Eagle had found their soulmates. Wyatt didn't begrudge any member of the team their happiness. They found the kind of companionship that thrived in this environment, which wasn't easy to do. Their jobs often required them to be gone for weeks at a time, much like when they'd been in the military.

Not to mention bullets still came whizzing by their heads.

"I got nothing better to do," Wyatt said.

"We'll meet you over there." Hunter nodded as the three men double-timed it toward the parking lot.

These were Wyatt's people. He'd be lost without each and every single man on Team Eagle. They were as cohesive as a team could be. They worked together as one unit and there was never any doubt who had his back.

Booker glanced over his shoulder before turning his attention to Wyatt. "Are you going to tell Kirby how you feel when she gets here?"

About a month ago—in a drunken haze—Wyatt had spilled his guts to his best friend. It wasn't news to Booker. He'd been picking on Wyatt about his feelings for Kirby since before the crash, but if Wyatt couldn't admit it to himself, he couldn't say the words to anyone else, including Booker.

Slowly, Wyatt stood. His legs held his weight. Holding his breath, he took two steps, praying he didn't have to sit back down. "I don't know," he admitted. In his mind, he'd gone over how to express his feelings to Kirby a million times. He'd played out how the conversation would go and all the possible outcomes.

But there were only two that mattered.

Either she wanted him in the forever kind of way.

Or she didn't.

It was the latter that terrified him because if she didn't, he really needed to end things and find a way to get over Kirby.

"You'll never know if you don't tell her." Booker slapped him on the shoulder and squeezed as they made their way across the hanger at a snail's pace. "She could be thinking the same thing you are."

"And what's that?"

Booker sighed, shaking his head. "Do I really need to spell this out for you, man?"

"Yes." Wyatt could use all the advice and insight he could get, even if he'd heard it before, and not just from Booker. Callie had gotten in on it too.

"For fuck's sake, man. You've been friends with benefits for like seven years." Booker held up his hand, shutting Wyatt up before he could go into all the reasons why. "I understand why it started that way. You were deployed with your SEAL team more than you were Stateside. You'd just become a team leader and you were focused on your career. You'd worked damn fucking hard to get to that position. It's all you'd ever wanted and having a committed girlfriend would have complicated things. Shortly after, she'd started working with her gorillas in the Congo. A real relationship with her had disaster written all over it at the time. But seriously, man. The two of you have lasted this long with a stupid rule of being honest about other people in your lives, and how many women have you been with? How many men has she been with? Come on. One of you needs to make the first move."

"She lives in fucking Africa. That hasn't changed. And she always tells me how great our *arrangement* is. How stress free it is for her with her job. She doesn't want to have an entanglement like a real boyfriend."

"You don't know that because you have never

once asked for more. You're just as bad as she is when it comes to your inability to commit. She could be afraid too."

"I'm not scared." Only he was fucking terrified of being rejected.

And of losing her forever.

"I call bullshit on that." Booker pushed open the door that led to the parking lot. "But dude, it's time to shit or get off the pot. You've got to tell her. I'm tired of how miserable this whole thing is making you. Trust me, no matter what happens, you will be relieved to have put it out there."

"Trust you? Like the time you tried to teach me how to fly? Jesus, man, I thought I was going to fucking die that day."

Booker paused and clenched his fists.

Fuck. "Wrong choice of words." Wyatt knew better than to toss *die* and *fly* in the same sentence. "I didn't mean it like that. I went Navy because I feel more comfortable on a boat in the middle of the ocean than I do in the air."

Booker laughed. "Then why the fuck did you follow me into an Aviation Division with this outfit?"

"You know the answer to that one."

"Maybe I need reminding." The tension in Booker's face eased, but it wasn't gone.

Ever since Wyatt had met Booker, their friendship had been more of a kinship. Brothers in the family sense of the word. Not to mention they had saved each other's ass more than once. If it wasn't for Booker, Wyatt would be dead.

The same was true in reverse.

"I better be your fucking best man when you make an honest woman out of Callie." Wyatt lowered his chin. It wasn't necessary to give Booker all the reasons why because the words didn't express their bond.

"Might be happening sooner rather than later." Booker arched a brow. "And she doesn't have too many girlfriends here and could be looking for a maid of honor, so get that ugly ass in gear and tell Kirby how you feel."

"You're a fucking pain in my ass, you know that?" Wyatt yanked open the driver's door of his Jeep. "I won't be able to drink much thanks to that medication. Maybe one beer, so feel free to get smashed tonight."

"Nope. I've got a warm body in my bed and I don't want to risk being turned down because I've had one too many." Booker climbed into the passenger seat, reached over, and patted Wyatt's leg. "A single beer and you're taking me home."

"You're pathetic."

"I'm a man in love."

Wyatt's phone buzzed. He pulled it out and glanced at the text.

Kirby: *I'm on a flight out of DC at 7 p.m. If I make it. Still have a few things to deal with. I'll text you if I get on* *the plane. I land in Bozeman at 11:30. I'll rent a car. Leave the door open. :)*

He set his cell in the cupholder and put the Jeep in reverse. At least she was coming. As long as he didn't get another migraine and his boss, Stone, didn't send him off on an assignment, the next few days should prove to lift his spirits.

That was until he had *the conversation.*

CHAPTER 2

Kirby Carrington covered her mouth. She'd counted eight yawns in the last half hour. She yanked her backpack from the passenger seat and tossed it over her shoulder. She'd snag her bigger one from the trunk in the morning. Right now, all she wanted to do was crawl into bed, wrap her arms and legs around Wyatt, and forget about her problems.

Someone on her team had royally fucked up and no one was taking responsibility for it. She could handle mistakes. They happened all the time. She could forgive that, but she couldn't forgive the lack of ownership by the person who had screwed up. The bigger problem was she knew exactly who had put in the order. Their damn name was on the paperwork.

Not to mention he was always the person who took care of supplies.

Ben had been working with her for the last three

years. He was almost as meticulous as her regarding the gorillas and their care. Making sure the team had the proper supplies and medicine had been his job and he hadn't once let her down.

Until now.

She made her way up the path toward Wyatt's pint-size cabin in West Yellowstone. The size of it made her chuckle considering Wyatt wasn't a small man. He stood six foot two and weighed at least two hundred and twenty pounds of solid muscle. He was broad. Thick. Everything she'd never been attracted to. When she was younger, she went for the nerdy guy. The bookworm. The man who loved science, biology, or better yet, animals. She always pictured herself marrying a veterinarian, or someone like her who studied different kinds of animals. Someone she could share her passion with.

Not a decorated sailor who dedicated his life to serving his country. Even out of the military, he found a way to make a difference and that's one of the reasons she found it impossible to let him go, when she should.

She blinked. At thirty-nine years old, she was burned-out. She had lived in the Congo for five years after completing her PhD in Psychology (Animal Behavior). She hadn't expected to live there that long. Gorillas weren't the only animal that she'd wanted to study. Wolves were another species that had always fascinated her. However, after two years working under some of the best people in the field, she was offered the lead position and the opportunity to write a book. She couldn't turn that down and she loved the gorillas. She'd become close to two gorilla families and had done some fantastic work.

But her book was completed. She had an offer from a prestigious publisher and her grant had expired. In six months, her time in the Congo would come to an end and Kirby would have to find something else to do, but she had no idea what. She'd dedicated so much of her life to researching and studying gorillas she'd forgotten about all the other things she'd been passionate about.

Including the wolf and Yellowstone National Park.

And then there was Wyatt.

The front door opened. "Hey, Kirby. You made good time." Wyatt took her bag. "Is there anything else from the car I can get?" He leaned in and kissed her cheek. Half the time they acted as if they were a couple. It was easy to be with him because he never made it weird for her to walk away. He never asked her to stay, mostly because he was always being shipped off to places he couldn't even tell her about.

However, they always managed to come together whenever they both had downtime. His move to West Yellowstone made it even easier since she always went to Utah whenever she came Stateside to visit her family.

Her fucking parents. God, she didn't want to see them this trip. Things hadn't gone well after the anniversary party. Once again, she had confronted her father and he lied to her face, like he always had.

And then there was her mother who enjoyed pretending her life was perfect, when in reality, it was far from it.

Of course, her folks enjoyed getting on her case about her life choices, reminding her of her past. Sometimes she wondered if her parents even liked her. She hightailed it back to the Congo and didn't communicate with them until a few weeks ago. She hadn't planned on making the medical supply run at the time, so they had no idea she was even in the country. Now that she was, she needed to decide if she would see them after spending a few days with Wyatt.

But Wyatt wasn't her boyfriend. He was a man she enjoyed sleeping with and occasionally, they had good conversation. They never fought because they didn't go deep. The only time she could say they even remotely had an argument had been five months ago about the damn fucking poachers, but only because Wyatt had been worried for her safety and damn, that felt good.

Her parents were more concerned with the fact she was pushing forty and wasn't married and hadn't provided them with a grandchild.

"It can wait until tomorrow, but I could use a bathroom," she said. "I need a shower."

"You know where it is. There are clean towels in the closet, and you left behind your body wash, shampoo, and conditioner last time you were here. It's all ready and waiting."

"Do you have any—"

"A pair of shorts and a T-shirt are hanging on the hooks."

"You're amazing." She scurried through the main room, which was the kitchen and the family room all wrapped into one. The only other room was his bedroom, which also housed the only bathroom. She closed the door and quickly turned on the shower to the hottest setting possible. She had no idea why she got nervous every time she saw him. They'd been doing this song and dance for years. It was comfortable and exactly what she needed.

Or so she told herself.

Only, things for her had changed the moment she got the phone call telling her he'd been in a helicopter crash. He downplayed his injuries, but they were bad enough that he left the military and they still plagued him today. The thought she could have lost him sent her into a fit of tears. She couldn't book herself on a charter to the States fast enough.

However, things between them remained the same.

They were still best friends who fucked.

Not that she minded. She'd been the one who set the boundary in the first place, but Wyatt didn't argue, plead, or try to renegotiate the arrangement.

Quickly, she shed herself of her dirty clothes that smelled of five days of airplane. She stepped under the glorious hot water and let it pelt her body. It felt like a little piece of heaven.

She lathered herself, thinking about all the ways Wyatt would fulfill her wildest dreams. Her skin sizzled. The anticipation was too much. She turned off the water, found the towel, and dried herself before finding the toothbrush she'd left behind the last time. Her heart fluttered, a little surprised he hadn't tossed it, but she wasn't about to read anything into it because Wyatt didn't like to waste anything. He was the kind of man who recycled religiously. He didn't order more than he needed and he gave to the poor every chance he got. He thought about others before he thought about himself.

When she stepped into the bedroom, he was turning down the sheets.

"Are you hungry? Thirsty?" he asked.

"Only for you." She shimmied out of her shorts and tossed them to the chair in the corner of the room. "You are a sight for sore eyes."

He ripped his shirt over his head and climbed onto the mattress. "What was the drama with your supplies?"

"They were incomplete and set for the wrong

date, as in four weeks from now." She eased in next to his taut, muscular body. She'd never met anyone quiet like Wyatt before. He was sexy as hell. Came off like a total Alpha, which should be a turnoff since she couldn't stand a chest-pounding kind of man. However, Wyatt had this soft, sweet, sensitive side that not everyone got to see. But he showed it to her and she soaked it up like the sweet, warm rays of the sun. "They will be there next week when I return to DC to fly back to Africa."

"I'm glad you were able to fix it." He pulled her to his chest, kissing her temple. "What about the poachers? What's going on with them?"

"Can we have this conversation tomorrow?"

He took her chin with his thumb and forefinger. "Humor me for a hot minute."

"Poachers will always be a problem, you know that." She ran her hand across his stomach, inching her fingers into the elastic of his flannel pants. "But it's been quiet where I am for the last few months since we shut down that one ring."

"Good. But that doesn't stop me from worrying about you. I watched that movie. *Gorillas of the Mist* or something."

She kissed his neck, darting her tongue out right under his earlobe.

He hissed, running his fingers through her wet hair.

"That's just a movie," she whispered.

"Based on a true story not far from your location."

"Next, you'll tell me that your job isn't dangerous." She straddled his legs, lifting her shirt over her head.

"Not the point." He reached behind her back, unhooking her bra, tickling her back with his fingers. "You're always acting like what happens out there doesn't affect you, when it does."

"Tell me this." She pressed her hands on his firm chest. "When was the last time you were shot at?" She ran a finger over one of his newer scars. It had been there the last time they were together, but that didn't change the facts. "Don't lie and don't give me details. Just answer the question."

"Two weeks ago," he said.

"I'd say you're more at risk for being killed than I am. So, can we please move past this conversation? It's been five months since I've had sex with anything other than a vibrator and while that's certainly enjoyable, it's not you or this." She reached inside his pajama bottoms and curled her fingers around his length.

Swiftly, he flipped her on her back and yanked her panties to her ankles. "You'll tell me all about doing that. I've seen you touch yourself, but you won't send me pictures when you're gone. Why not?"

"Would you send me some?"

"Absolutely not." He kissed her navel. His hands roamed her body. "You know I hate having my picture taken. Why would I enjoy doing a naked selfie."

She burst out laughing. "God, I've missed you."

He kissed his way up to her lips. "You've missed me?" He fanned her hair from her face. "Or you've missed sex with me?"

Staring into his deep, dark eyes, she couldn't find her voice. She swallowed, hard. In all the years she'd known him, he'd never asked her that question. Or one like it and she wasn't sure how to respond to it. He could often be sarcastic, but his tone gave away nothing.

He pressed his lips on the center of her chest. His hands cupped her breasts. His thumbs fanned over her hard nipples, making it impossible to concentrate, much less form a sentence. Maybe his question had been rhetorical. Anything was possible and she decided to enjoy the moment over cluttering it up with more chatter.

His fingers slid between her legs, teasing and torturing her while his hot breath hovered over her like a warm breeze rolling in off the ocean. He was everything she could have imagined in a lover. Tender and wild at the same time. If she could ever give herself fully to a man, it would be Wyatt.

But people couldn't be trusted.

Both men and women.

That lesson had been engraved in her DNA from

when she caught her father cheating on her mother when she was twelve years old.

She pushed those thoughts from her brain and focused on the pleasure that only Wyatt could bring her body and mind. It was easy to forget about all her problems. None of which she needed to deal with right away. The supplies had been handled and she didn't need to focus on the next chapter in her life until this one was over.

There was no reason to rush out and look for another job or research grant. She could take some time and travel or relax.

She arched, begging for him to go deeper. Harder. Faster.

His tongue lapped against her in soft strokes, making her dizzy. Her toes curled as she dug her heels into the mattress. The tension filled her muscles. Her breath came in short, choppy pants. Rolling her hips with the motion of his fingers and mouth, her orgasm rippled across her body like massive waves breaking against the shore over and over again.

Braiding her fingers through his hair, she tugged.

He lifted his head, licking his lips.

She quivered.

Kissing her stomach, he eased himself on top of her, reaching for the nightstand.

God, she hated condoms, but they were a necessary evil. Having children hadn't been on her radar. It wasn't that she didn't believe in family, because she did. She'd seen others have success with marriage and children, but Kirby's life experiences showed her the opposite.

Wyatt rolled the protection over himself before lacing his fingers through hers and easing himself inside. He kept his torso from touching hers as he gently and slowly filled her with passionate strokes. He stared into her eyes with desire and something that could be mistaken for adoration.

She wrapped her legs tightly around his waist, drawing him in as deep as possible. She needed him tonight more than ever. He not only represented the physical connection to the real world, but if she could ever pull her head out of her ass, he could hold the key to her future.

He leaned over, taking her nipple into his mouth and sucking hard.

"Oh, God, yes." Her skin felt as though it burst into flames. Her climax collided with his as he thrust inside her with force. Not once. Not twice. But four times.

Her stomach muscles convulsed with the purest form of delight she'd ever experienced. She grappled to fill her lungs with oxygen as he collapsed on top of her, shifting slightly to the side, kissing her neck, whispering sweet words in her ear.

There was so much she didn't know about Wyatt, and yet, she felt more connected to him than anyone else in her life. Their conversations weren't overly intense.

The discussions they had were all related to their work. He told her about his training. His love of the water. His reasons for joining the Navy. His passion for being a SEAL.

She shared her joys of being with animals and told him all about the gorilla families she had met in the Congo.

Occasionally, they leaned on each other regarding the tougher issues in life, but they always managed to keep each other at arm's length when it came to the real deep emotional stuff.

They would text back and forth about their hobbies outside of work. How he loved to hike and kayak and she did too. They both loved reading, though their interests in that were vastly different. He liked nonfiction about history and she preferred anything to do with animals.

He rolled to the side, pulling her close, kissing her temple. "It's good to see you again."

"You as well." She rested her chin on his chest. "I can only stay a couple of days. I've got to go visit my family even though they make me crazy."

"I figured," he said. "Can you at least stay through the weekend so we can have a whole day together? I've got training and a medical thing I've got to do."

She jerked her head. "Medical? What's wrong?"

"Aw, are you concerned about me?"

"Don't be a dick." She poked his pec. "Are you getting migraines again?"

"Just one, but that requires me to have a physical."

"At least you're not lying about it." She rested her head on his shoulder.

"I might be cocky, arrogant, and even a bit of a thrill seeker, but I'd like to live out the remainder of my days with my brain functioning and mostly at optimal capacity."

"You really should hear yourself sometime."

He chuckled. "Just stretching my mind with words." He tucked her back to his chest. "Now get some sleep. I'm sure you're exhausted."

"You have no idea," she said. "What time do you need to leave for work?"

"Early. Oh, and we're having dinner with Booker and Callie tomorrow night at their place."

"I look forward to it." Taking in a deep breath, she closed her eyes. Eventually, she would need to have a conversation with Wyatt, but not until she knew what she wanted to do next. Until she had a handle on that, there was no reason to discuss changing anything about their *arrangement*. The last thing she wanted to do was scare the man.

CHAPTER 3

WYATT JERKED AWAKE. He reached for his cell, assuming the obnoxious ring was his phone telling him it was time to wake up. Unusual for him since he usually woke a good half hour before his alarm went off.

But that sound wasn't his.

"Kirby." He poked her arm. "Someone's calling you." He rubbed his eyes and glanced at the time. Shit. It was four thirty in the morning. He'd never be able to go back to sleep now. He stretched, thinking of at least one activity he could enjoy before heading to work. He wrapped his arms around his naked houseguest, pressing his lips against her shoulder.

"Hello?" Kirby batted his hands from her breasts. "Ben? I can barely hear you. The line is full of static." She pushed herself to a sitting position, shoving him back to his side of the bed.

That didn't help his ego.

"Do you mind if I put this on speaker to see if it helps?" she whispered.

"Go right ahead." He leaned back, clasping his hands behind his head. He could be patient and wait for the call to be over. Hopefully, it wouldn't last long and her mood wouldn't be too soured.

She tapped the screen. "Ben? Can you hear me?"

Crackle. Crackle. Static.

"Kirby... Oh... God... bzzzzzzz... mess... bzzzzz... Tav... bzzzz... bloody... bzzzz... no one left."

Wyatt bolted to a sitting position. "Ben, this is Wyatt Bixby with the Brotherhood Protectors. Can you repeat that, please?"

Kirby glared, as if to tell him to stand down. "Ben? Can you hear me? What's going on?"

"Bzzzzz... Tav and... bzzzzz... The team... bzzzzz..." The line cut out.

Kirby lifted her cell and frantically tapped at the screen. "Fuck, it's going straight to voicemail."

"Try again," Wyatt said in a calm voice. He rested his hand on her thigh and squeezed while he formulated his own plan.

She sucked in a deep breath and hit the callback button. This time a beeping noise came over the speaker. "Goddammit."

"Set it aside and wait for five minutes. He might be trying to reach you."

She jerked her head and gave him the stink eye. "Did we not just hear the same conversation?"

If looks could kill, he'd be six feet under. "Isn't Tav one of your alpha gorillas?" He needed to keep her as peaceful as possible while he organized his thoughts. A dozen scenarios played out in rapid succession in his brain, but only two made sense.

The first one wasn't horrible, but she would have a different opinion.

The second one made his heart thump faster and the blood in his veins boil.

She nodded. "He's close to six feet tall and remember I told you he's a legend in the area. Everyone thought we should pack up and move when he showed up near camp. It was rumored that he's killed at least a half dozen men. I don't believe it, except if anyone tried to harm his family. I could see him turning against even my team whom he's learned to trust." She pounded her sweet little fingers against her cell.

Same annoying beeping sound.

He curled his fingers around her wrist. "Dumb question, but how is Ben reaching you from the Congo?"

"I'm assuming he's connecting through our satcom. He's a cyber geek, kind of like you."

Wyatt groaned. "I was communications and intelligence before I became a SEAL team leader. Just because my degree was in cyber operations doesn't make me… never mind." He knew his IQ and he got he was a fucking genius, something he tried to forget. He skated through college without even trying. The only thing that challenged him at the Naval Academy had been the physical aspect and the part where he'd been told he could never make it as a SEAL. Having entered college as a scrawny young man who preferred books over anything else, but had this idea that he wanted to be the best of the best, he took his entire life as a challenge. He pushed himself hard and did what everyone thought was impossible. "Let me call Booker and we'll head into the office."

"For what?"

"I've got state-of-the-art equipment. We can call Ben back from there. It will be a much better connection. I might be able to redirect a satellite and get a picture of his location so we can see what's going on."

She leaped from the bed, gathering up a shirt and shorts.

He blinked, doing his best to focus on anything but her naked body.

"You can do all that?" she asked.

He cocked his head. "I'm the best at what I do."

"I thought all you did was follow Booker."

"Ouch. That hurt." He narrowed his eyes. "For the record, I was Navy. He was Flight Concept Division. Two totally different things. He was my transport to many a mission…" Wyatt sighed. He had no idea why he felt the need to explain or defend his friendship with Booker, especially to Kirby.

"I was just teasing you." She pulled the long shirt over her head. "I need to know what's happening with my team and gorillas. Any chance we can leave now?"

"I need to get approval for you to be in the office, but that won't take but a phone call." He slipped from the bed, finding his pajama bottoms. He never used to wear them, but West Yellowstone in the middle of winter was damn fucking cold. "I'm going to go put on a pot of coffee because I won't be able to function and I did have a migraine yesterday, so I need to do whatever I can to ward off another one."

She grabbed his arm. "How bad?"

"It only lasted ten minutes." He kissed her temple. "Come on. I've got two phone calls to make. In the meantime, why don't you try to text Ben. Tell him to be near the comms."

"Okay." She nodded. "Thanks."

"What are friends for." He turned, snagged his cell, and tried not to cringe at the word *friend* when in reality he wanted so much more. However, for now, that's what they were and this wasn't the time to have a different conversation.

He placed his phone to his ear.

"This better be fucking good," Booker said with a snarl.

"I need you to meet me at the office in twenty."

"Why the fuck would I do that?" Booker asked. "Better yet, why would you? Didn't Kirby show up?"

"Yeah. She's here, and she's the one who needs our help." Wyatt stuffed a large travel mug under his coffee maker and pushed the largest button. The machine gurgled to life. He reached for his medication, which he kept to the right of the sink and popped it into his mouth before turning on the faucet and sticking his face in the running water. He swallowed.

"Help? What for?"

"I'm not exactly sure, but it sounds like her team back in the Congo could be in trouble."

"Fucking poachers," Booker mumbled. "What happened?"

"That's just it. I have no idea. I couldn't understand her assistant. What I did hear, I didn't like. I need to get into my office so I can reach him via satellite hookup and I need to do it ASAP. But first I have to get Stone to allow Kirby access."

"I'll handle Stone. See you in a half hour tops." The line went dead.

Wyatt pulled down another travel mug, placed it under the spout of the coffee maker, and hit the start button. "Be ready to roll in five minutes." He raked a hand across the top of his head and meandered into the bedroom.

"I'm ready now." She hiked up the jeans she'd been wearing the night before.

"That's my flannel. What if I had been planning on wearing that today?"

"You have twenty of these." She lifted her hand over her shoulder and thumbed toward the closet. "Black T-shirts in the summer and red, black, green, or orange flannels in the winter. You're pathetic."

"I'm a creature of habit, is what I am." Gently, he shoved her out of the way and snagged a shirt along with a pair of black denims. "And every time you come to visit, I end up missing one or two."

"They're comfortable." She pulled her long blond hair into a ponytail on the top of her head. "I will need my computer in my smaller backpack."

"Grab whatever." He sat on the edge of the bed and pulled socks onto his feet. "I noticed all you had was a fleece. You'll swim in my jackets, but it will be better than nothing."

"Thanks." She pulled one from his closet. "I will take you up on that."

"But it's not for you to steal."

She put her arms into the sleeves. Her hands disappeared. "You don't have to worry about that with this thing. It's ugly and you could fit two of me in this."

He laughed. "You can do the same thing with my shirts."

"Yeah, but they're great for nightshirts." She winked. "Are you ready yet? Jeez, you take freaking forever."

"Let's go." He took her by the hand.

"Thank you."

"For what?"

"Joking around and keeping me distracted." She followed him to the Jeep. "I'm really worried."

"I know you are." He cradled her chin in his hand. "I'll do whatever it takes to help you regain communications with your team."

~

Kirby tossed Wyatt's oversized coat on the small sofa in the corner of his office. "This is impressive." She ran her finger across his massive desk with a picture of him and the rest of Team Eagle. She'd known Booker for as long as she'd been with Wyatt. The rest of his team, she'd met first right after the crash and then a couple of times after that when visiting.

All good men. The best.

"What is it with these screens?" A second desk on the back wall housed five screens and a computer.

"Did you seriously just ask me that?" He waved to the chair on the side of his desk while he made himself comfortable in his big leather one, turning his back. When he fired up his computer, all the screens came to life. "I need your satcom information."

A tap at the door startled her and she jumped, dropping her bag on her foot. "Shit," she mumbled.

"I'm sorry. Didn't mean to scare you," a man she'd never met before said.

"Hey, Stone." Wyatt leaped around his desk, stretching out his hand. "It wasn't my intention to get you out of bed this early in the morning."

"Not a problem." Stone nodded.

"This is Kirby Carrington," Wyatt said. "She's an animal behaviorist working in the Congo. She had a strange communication with her assistant this morning that got disconnected and we haven't been able to—"

"Booker has read me in on what happened. I thought I'd come in and see if I can help." Stone lowered himself onto the couch. "Or better yet, watch the master do his thing and maybe learn something."

Wyatt chuckled.

"Hank hired a team in Colorado. One of the men specializes in computer programming and cyber shit. He comes from the Army and JSOC. His name is Darius Ford," Stone said.

"I know Darius." Wyatt swiveled in his chair while his fingers glided across the keyboard like two people doing the tango. "We met on a joint assignment about ten years ago. He makes me look stupid when it comes to programming and hacking. He's got a unique and mesmerizing coding style."

"Yo, Kirby. You look fantastic." Callie bolted into the office with her arms wide.

Kirby jumped from the chair and wrapped her arms around the woman she'd only met a handful of times. However, it felt as though they were old friends. "Living in Montana seems to agree with you." Kirby looked Callie up and down. "I hope Booker isn't being too much of an ass." She glanced over her shoulder. "And that one isn't sticking his nose where it doesn't belong."

Callie laughed. "Like I'd have it any other way."

"Hey, Kirby." Booker kissed her on the cheek. "It's good to see you."

"You as well." She gave him a weak smile. The longer they stood there shooting the shit, the faster her heart pounded in her chest.

"Kirby, I need your phone." Wyatt held out his hand. "Booker, get me the comms kit from my closet."

"Sure thing." Booker strolled across the room with the same sense of confidence he'd always had. Kirby admired that. From the moment she met Booker, she understood his connection with Wyatt, which many thought strange. The two men were like a set of twins. It was if they'd been separated at birth. They didn't need to explain their bond—it just was and anyone in their life, especially a woman, had to either understand it or accept it.

Callie had no problem with Wyatt and Booker.

Nor did Kirby, only Kirby and Wyatt weren't a couple. They were barely a thing.

Friends who fucked.

She cringed at the thought.

Hooked up?

No. That didn't work anymore either.

For seven years the fact they had never defined their relationship had been what made it work. Now it's what made her nervous.

She handed him her cell and two seconds later, Booker set what looked like a small suitcase on the desk and opened it. Booker helped Wyatt connect it to his computer.

It wasn't like she didn't know how to use a satcom connection, but some of it was beyond her pay grade.

"Okay. We're all set to make the call." Wyatt set her phone to the side. "I can put it on my computer speakers so we can all hear."

Stone leaned forward on the sofa. Callie sat next to him and Booker leaned his ass against the main desk.

"You can sit here." Wyatt stood, offering his big leather chair while he stood behind it.

The connection buzzed, making noise much like an old dial-up internet connection from the early nineties.

She placed her palms on the desk and took in a slow calming breath. It had been an hour since the first call had come in from Ben.

"Hello?" Ben's weak voice crackled over the speaker. "Who's there?"

"Ben, it's Kirby. What's going on?"

He coughed, making a gurgling sound. "Kirby. It... *cough... gag... gag...* a massacre. They came... *gag... gurgle... gag...* from nowhere."

She could barely hear his faint whisper. She leaned closer to the speaker. "Where are you? Are you hurt?"

"I'm hiding not far from the camp," he managed through a fit of coughs. "I think I'm dying and everyone else is dead."

"I can try to pin his location." Wyatt squeezed her shoulder before reaching over her and tapping his fingers on his keyboard. "Ben, this is Wyatt, remember me?"

"Yeah," Ben said faintly.

"Can you tell me which direction you traveled from the camp and approximately how far away you are?"

"I went north... *gag... gurgle... gurgle... cough...* east. I couldn't tell you the distance." There was a long pause with silence.

"Ben? Are you still there?" Kirby asked with desperation laced in every syllable.

"Yes," Ben whispered.

"Hang tight, buddy. We'll get a rescue team to you." Wyatt pulled his keyboard closer. "I've got a general location. Keep the satphone with you."

"Suit up." Stone stood. "I'm sending your team in."

"I'm going too." Callie jumped to her feet.

"Negative," Stone said.

Callie planted her hands on her hips. "You could use someone like me."

"Are you asking for a job? Because I'd hire you." Stone cocked his head. "But even if I did, you wouldn't be going on this assignment."

"We're coming to get you, Ben," Kirby said into the phone.

"It will be too late," Ben whispered.

"Ben," Stone said with a commanding voice. "I'm Wyatt's boss. We've got connections and we'll get someone in the area as soon as possible. It won't be long. Team Eagle will be wheels up within the hour and we'll investigate the situation. Whatever happened there and whoever did this, we'll make sure justice is served." Stone nodded. "Call your men." He pointed at Booker. "The entire team is going in."

"Yes, sir." Booker nodded.

"Wyatt, get me Ben's location. I'll start making calls. There has to be someone we know close who can extract Ben and get him safely to the nearest American hospital." Stone turned on his heel and marched out of Wyatt's office.

"Did you hear that, Ben? It's going to be okay," Kirby said with her heart in her throat.

Nothing but static echoed over the comms.

"Ben," she repeated.

Still silence.

Tears burned a path down her cheek.

"We've got to roll." Wyatt lifted her from the chair. "I've got a charter plane lined up for us."

"Already?" She shifted her gaze. "How'd you do that so fast?"

"It's what we do." Wyatt took her by the hand. "We leave in forty minutes. Booker will still need to use our contacts to get us a helicopter and a guide once we land at the Kinshasa N'djili airport. But we can do all that in the air."

"I'm your guide," Kirby said.

Wyatt narrowed his eyes.

"I've lived there for five years. I know it like the back of my hand. We'll get there faster with me as our guide. Hiring a local, they will want to play it safe. They will take the long way to get there. Plus, I know an area closer to the site you can set down a bird where no one else would dare do it, except maybe you guys."

Booker glanced over his shoulder. "Is that because of the terrain or something else?"

"Mostly the terrain, but if poachers hit us and they see helicopters flying in, they could see that as a threat. Once we land, it's still a good two-hour hike to where we need to go. I know better than anyone how to get there."

"Maybe we should get two birds," Booker said. "Especially since we're taking the entire team and we'll have three pilots. We might be able to find a closer place to set the choppers down."

Kirby shook her head. "The closest town is three hours away. We hike down from the mountains where we have a place to store a Jeep. From there, we drive to town. The only place that would be safe is the clearing where we keep our vehicles and other things. The area is remote. The locals are used to me, but they won't like you. Even landing there could be seen as hostile."

"Stone will make sure the area is as secure as possible by the time we get there. I will need the coordinates for that clearing." Wyatt led her out of the office and down the hallway toward the main entrance of the building. The Aviation office was located not far outside of West Yellowstone at the Brotherhood Protectors private airstrip. "But two birds is a good idea. We won't be able to make a plan until we know what we're dealing with."

"That could be in the air on the way over." Booker looped an arm around Callie's hip. "There's an Army base not too far from that part of the Congo. There are always joint missions run out of there. I'm sure there's some special forces team that Stone will be able to call on."

Kirby swallowed the thick lump that had formed in her throat. It didn't move. "Ben had been scheduled to go on this run," she whispered.

Wyatt paused midstep. "When and why did you make the change?"

"My grant is up in six months. I had two meetings. One to meet my replacement. He'll be joining me in two months. The second was with the publisher for my book."

"That doesn't answer my question about when you made the decision to go instead of Ben?" Wyatt stared at her with his intense dark eyes. His forehead crinkled like it always did when that brain of his was working overtime. "Because you didn't tell me you were coming until two weeks ago."

"It was a day before I messaged you," she admitted. "I could have put off the publisher or done a Zoom call. I could have even waited for my replacement to show up in the Congo, but I didn't think Ben had a reason to be Stateside. I did." She held his gaze.

"Why didn't you tell me about your grant?" Wyatt asked. "And the fact that you'd be coming home in less than a year?"

That was a fucking loaded question and one she had no idea how to answer. So many things in her life were up in the air. When she'd graduated from college, she had no direction, thanks to an ex-boyfriend whom she allowed to strip her of her dignity and confidence. The only thing she knew she wanted to do was travel and study various animals and their relationship with community. "Because I don't know what's next and my work with the gorillas isn't done." She wanted to say more, but this was not the moment to do it.

Wyatt arched a brow but thankfully didn't say another word.

"Did you have any other communications with people about your return?" Booker asked.

She shook her head. "My family doesn't even know I'm here. I was going to surprise them." She left out the part where her dad got pissed off over Wyatt. It wasn't about her being involved with a man; it was the fact that she didn't define who Wyatt was to her and that annoyed her father because he didn't control the situation. Even though he'd never met him, he didn't like Wyatt because her father believed if Wyatt wasn't man enough to come around, he wasn't the kind of person she belonged with, but that wasn't the reason she didn't bring Wyatt home to meet her folks.

They didn't understand.

And truthfully, neither did she anymore, but not for the same reasons.

"So, what you're saying is other than a message to me through an app on your cell phone while you in a neighboring town, no one outside of your team knows you're in the States?" Wyatt let out a long breath.

She nodded.

"Are you thinking what I'm thinking?" Booker raked a hand across the top of his head.

"Fuck, yeah," Wyatt muttered.

"Someone want to fill me in on what the hell the Bobbsey Twins are mulling over in their shared brain?" Kirby glanced between the two men, before glaring at Callie, who shrugged.

"Don't look at me," Callie said. "I've never understood their connection and trust me, I've tried."

"You put poachers in jail, Kirby." Wyatt yanked open the main doors and pressed his hand on the small of her back. "While I'm glad you turned everything over to the authorities and the bastards were caught, I warned you it wasn't over."

"Poachers are part of the Congo. There's more than one group. They pop up all the time." She picked up the pace, heading toward his Jeep.

"Maybe so, but I did a little digging after the last time you were here, and that ring wasn't a small-time operation," Wyatt said. "They might be in jail, but that doesn't mean they don't have friends and won't seek revenge."

"Are you saying they were coming for me?" For five years she'd learned to live with a heavy dose of fear and not just from the fact her gorillas could have killed her if they wanted to. But poachers were always a threat. So were some of the locals. While most appreciated and respected her work, there were some who didn't. She was the interloper and a handful of people made it clear they didn't want her there.

"That's a real possibility." Wyatt rolled his neck. "Maybe you should stay right here. Or go to your parents' while we sort this out."

She poked him dead center in his chest. "Over my fucking dead body. That's my team. My gorillas. They are all my responsibility. If you think I'm going to sit on my ass—here in the States—you've got another thing coming, buddy." She jogged around the hood of the Jeep. "Callie, sorry to be taking your boyfriend away. We'll have dinner the next time I'm in town."

"You bet your butt we will." Callie waved. "You boys be safe." She gave Booker a big kiss. "Watch your back and make sure Wyatt doesn't do anything stupid."

"I never do." Wyatt climbed behind the steering wheel and took Kirby's hand. "What can I do to talk you out of this?"

"Nothing. Now drive," she said.

"You heard the lady." Booker shut the passenger door.

"You're not even going to back me on this?" Wyatt glanced over his shoulder.

"I know better." Booker grinned like a schoolboy. "Better get this hunk of metal in gear. The team has been called and everyone is heading to the main airport."

"Fuck. Fine," Wyatt said.

Kirby dropped her head back and closed her eyes.

Even with a direct flight to Africa, it would still take them twenty to twenty-four hours to get to the camp. She could only pray that a rescue team would find Ben and get him to a hospital before they landed.

She had no idea what they were walking into. All she knew was that she needed answers.

CHAPTER 4

Wyatt rubbed the back of his neck as he stared at the map sprawled out over the hood of the ancient Jeep. The temperature hit eighty. It wasn't overly humid, which was a pleasant surprise and a nice reprieve from the frigid temps of Montana.

But damn, the size of the insects was terrifying.

"Ben's in critical condition." Kirby tied her flannel around her waist and leaned against the vehicle next to Booker. "The doctor told me he was shot six times and lost so much blood he couldn't believe he was alive when the SEAL team brought him in." She swiped at her cheeks. "He doesn't know if he'll make it, though. If they can get him to a more stable condition, they want to transport to Germany."

"Do you want to go be by his side?" Wyatt squeezed her forearm. "We can get someone to take you to Camp Lemonnier."

"No. I need to go back to camp and see for myself what happened and check on my gorillas."

"You heard the report." Wyatt understood why she wanted to go. However, he'd prefer to save her from the pain of seeing the carnage. The report he'd been handed informed him that not all the bodies had been bagged and removed. Not to mention there were some decapitated gorillas in the area.

This would not go over well with Kirby.

"That SEAL team could be in danger from the gorillas. Especially Tav and his brothers. They are incredibly territorial and protective. They have taken on many of my team as their own kind. They might go on the attack if they weren't killed or taken."

"The men are well aware of that fact." Wyatt lifted his chin, waving to the rest of his team as they strolled across the tarmac.

"We've secured a small prop plane with a pilot that will take us to a town in this area." Gunnar tapped the map. "From there, we've got two birds. It will be a forty-minute flight to here." He used his finger to circle a section of the map. "Is there where we want to be?"

"Yes," Kirby said. "I know people in that village where we're picking up the helicopters. They can give us some insight on what's been happening with the poaching ring." She ran a finger through her long blond ponytail. "If people don't see all of us together, one of you might be able to pose as a buyer."

"Of what?" Xavier asked.

"Gorilla paws. Meat. Whatever." Kirby's mouth filled with bile. "There's always a foreigner looking for trophies or to try something gamey. It sickens me, but it happens. I can coach one of you on what to say and how to go about it without looking like an amateur buyer."

"I can handle that." Hunter raised his hand, wiggling his fingers.

"You're a dog lover. Hell, you love all animals," Gunn said. "How the hell are you going to pose as someone who is into that kind of thing?"

"That could work to his advantage," Kirby agreed. "If any of my gorillas have been killed. Most of their meat or parts have probably already been sold, but poachers will go back looking for more. If my team is dead, they will return and those selling on the streets will hint at when more could be coming."

"I've eaten some strange shit in my days," Xavier said. "But gorilla isn't one I'd want to try."

"I think we can all agree that's gross." Wyatt folded the map. "When does this plane leave and why isn't Booker flying it?"

Xavier and Hunter rolled their eyes.

"I'm just as good, if not better than that asshole," Xavier said.

"Never implied you weren't." Wyatt stuffed the map into his rucksack and tossed it over at Gunn. "But if I have to go up in the fucking air on something that isn't commercial or has rubber bands instead of jets, I do it with him."

"Well, the only way we're getting to the next airstrip in a timely manner is if we go with that guy over there." Gunn jerked his thumb in the direction of a toothless man with a funky grin. "You might want to close your eyes before getting on the plane. He might have built it himself."

"You can be a real dick sometimes," Wyatt muttered. He knew Gunn was busting his ass, but still. Wyatt had issues flying before the crash. When he'd been six years old, his uncle took him up in a homemade plane and scared the living shit out of him flying like a complete maniac. The next time he got up in the air he'd been eight and he bawled like a baby the entire time down to Florida. The flight attendants had been great and the pilots let him look inside the cockpit.

But it didn't help.

The only one who had ever been able to alleviate his fear of flying had been Booker, which didn't make sense. The man flew like a bat out of hell, not to mention they'd been in more than one crash together.

However, Booker had always been in control. He never pushed harder than he could handle. He was as cool as a cucumber in an emergency, and if Wyatt ever had to die in a plane, he would do it with Booker. That might be a strange thing to the rest of the world, but it made perfect fucking sense to Wyatt.

"But you love me anyway." Gunn smiled.

Wyatt let out a long breath. "Why don't you all go load up our shit on that hunk of tin and we'll be over in a minute."

"Wheels up in fifteen." Xavier slapped him on the back before walking away with the rest of the team.

A local man and woman strolled by, pausing briefly.

The woman stared at Kirby, gasping. "She alive. She alive." The woman pointed frantically.

The man scowled. "Not possible." He grabbed the woman by the arm and scurried on past.

"That's the second time that's happened," Kirby said as she pulled out her phone and tapped at the screen. "It's as if people around here all assumed I died with everyone else on my team."

"That makes me worry that this wasn't about gorillas."

"It's always about them. Between the poachers and the rich people wanting their trophies and exotic meat. And then there's the fact developers are displacing the gorillas and they end up coming in contact with more and more humans who don't know how to behave around them. It's putting the population in danger." She stared at her cell with a perplexed look on her face.

"Is everything okay?"

"Yeah. Just stuff about my grant that needs to be dealt with later," she said.

Wyatt took her by the hand. "I want to get a few things straight before we get on the aircraft."

"I don't like the sound of that." She narrowed her stare. She'd never been the kind of woman who liked being told what to do or how to do it, especially by a man. Kirby was fiercely independent. It was one of the things that drew him to her in the first place.

He had no doubt she could handle herself in almost any given situation.

But this was different.

They had no idea who they were dealing with or what they wanted, but Wyatt had a bad feeling that these fuckers wanted Kirby and they weren't going to stop until they finished the job.

"I understand that we're in your backyard now. I've never been deployed in this area before and we will need your expertise. But make no mistake, we're in charge. What we say goes and I need to know that you will follow our instructions, without question."

She pursed her lips.

Never a good sign.

"I'm not kidding, Kirby. You may believe this is another poaching, but what if it's something bigger than that? What if whoever came to your camp didn't go there just for the gorillas?"

"You've already made that theory abundantly clear." She held up her hand. "I'm not disagreeing that it could be the case. But the local government would have informed me of any chatter they heard if that were true."

He closed his eyes for a count of five before blinking. "Because the politics here aren't corrupt."

"There are people who want to ensure the gorillas are protected." She planted her hands on her hips. "They don't want to see the mountain gorillas become extinct, and that is what will happen if this continues."

"That's all good and probably true. But all it takes is one slimy politician to take a bribe. Not to mention that this area is being built up. Gorillas are being displaced as more land is developed. That pushes them into defense mode." He pressed his finger over her mouth. "I did some research and I've read about gorillas attacking people not all that far from your basecamp. Progress often takes precedence over things like protecting local wildlife, whether we like it or not."

She let out a sarcastic laugh, shaking her head. "You're missing my point."

"I don't think I am," he said. "All the government officials you're dealing with might say they want to protect the gorillas, and maybe they do, but they need to protect what the people they are serving want more. That's income and the opportunity for growth. A few dead gorillas is a trade-off. To them, it's not the end of the world. They most likely don't believe the species will ever become extinct."

"Then they're stupid."

"I'm not disagreeing with you. But my job now is to find out what happened and to keep you safe. I can't do that if I'm worried you're going to go off and do something crazy. So, please, promise me you'll follow my orders."

"I'm not a soldier in this outfit."

"Neither are any of us." He inched closer, lifting her chin with his thumb and forefinger. "Order was the wrong word choice."

"And what would be a better one?"

"Directive?"

"Fine," she said. "But you have to promise that when it comes to the gorillas, you have to listen to everything I say because when we come across them —and we will—you and your team will be in big trouble if you don't follow my *directives*."

"That's fair enough." He palmed her cheek.

"You're seriously not going to kiss me with your entire team looking on, are you? Because that wouldn't be professional."

"Are you going to stop me?" The corners of his mouth tugged into a slight smile as he brushed his lips across hers in a tender kiss. It was quick and not overly romantic, but it got the job done.

She pressed her hand in the center of his chest. "Everyone is staring."

"You think I care?" He winked. "It's not like they all don't know."

"Know what, exactly?" she asked. "Never mind. I don't want you to answer that."

He laughed, pressing his hand against the small of her back. "Come on. Time to fly the not-so-friendly skies." God, he hated flying. The closer he got to the plane that looked as though someone took a sledgehammer to it, the more he wished there was some boat they could take. Water was so much better. He'd rather deal with the angry ocean than even the smoothest of air.

"Take my hand." He helped her onto the rickety steps. His heart thumped in the center of his chest as he climbed into the small prop plane. All he could think about was the fact that the props were held together by rubber bands and hoped they didn't snap. A visual that played out in his brain like a bad horror movie.

He took a seat—if one could call the fold-down metal contraptions seats—next to Booker with Kirby on his other side.

Xavier, Gunn, and Hunter were across on the other side.

He strapped himself in, checking the durability of the harness. He wasn't sure he'd been in a worse aircraft, but he sure as shit had been in more dangerous situations.

Bullets had flown by his head more than once.

He'd been shot six times.

That hadn't been a walk in the park.

Two helicopter crashes, both with Booker as the pilot. The first one hadn't been horrible. Terrifying, but Booker had managed to land the bird without too much difficulty after losing power in a field. They'd hit the ground hard and fast, but the injuries to himself, and everyone on board, had been minimal.

The second one had been life-altering for Team Eagle and had killed good men, not to mention it had fundamentally changed Booker. The overwhelming responsibility the man felt for the team still haunted Booker to this day. It shouldn't. What happened wasn't Booker's fault. However, Wyatt understood Booker better than anyone and didn't dare belittle his emotions. Booker was still the best damn pilot and Wyatt didn't want to fly with anyone else unless he was given no other choice.

Which unfortunately happened a little too often.

Like in this moment.

The hunk of a death trap rattled to life.

"We're ready for takeoff." The pilot glanced over his shoulder and smiled a toothless grin. The fucker looked as if he was ninety with his wrinkled face, beady eyes, and haggard expression.

The aircraft eased from its position toward the short runway.

Wyatt sucked in a deep breath and ran his hands up and down his legs.

"Are you okay?" Kirby asked.

Booker leaned over and whispered in her ear.

Wyatt could only hear every other word over the loud engines, but he got enough of Booker's words so that he knew he wouldn't have to respond to Kirby's question.

She shifted her gaze between Booker and Wyatt.

"Are you kidding me?" she asked softly.

Fuck. The last thing he needed was for anyone to bring attention to his aversion to flying, especially during takeoff. That was the worst fucking part next to the actual flying in the air. The turbulence, which was always worse in a small plane. And then the landing, although that part he could handle as long as there wasn't a malfunction.

Or turbulence.

Or Kirby staring at him like he was a freak of nature.

"What?" He glared.

"Nothing," she mumbled, shifting her gaze to her lap. The corners of her mouth tipped into a tiny smile.

"I'm so glad you find this amusing." He rolled his neck, focusing on Hunter, who gave him a slight head nod, as if that would reassure him, but it least it was a nonjudgmental friendly face.

"It's just that I didn't know this about you." She picked at her thumbnail. "I mean, you had no problem on the commercial flight."

"I usually don't."

The plane made the turn onto the runway and immediately picked up speed.

He closed his eyes.

"That's weird," she said.

"No stranger than your fear of cockroaches."

"They're nasty fucking creatures," she yelled over the roar of the engines. "They scatter the second the lights come on and that's just creepy as fuck."

Wyatt chuckled, recalling a memory of her clinging to him in the kitchen of a rental they'd stayed at for a long weekend while he'd been doing a training exercise at Coronado Naval Base in California. "Maybe you should study their community habits."

"Oh, aren't you a funny man."

His stomach flipped upside down and sideways as the plane lifted into the air and banked right a little faster than he believed was appropriate. He blinked, needing to get his bearings. He could handle rough seas all day long, but this made him fucking crazy. At least this would be a short flight and the next one he could be in the cockpit with Booker. That would at least give him a sense of control.

The therapist the military and the Brotherhood Protectors had required him to see believed some of his issues with flying had to do with not having a sense of being in charge. While he didn't discount the idea, it struck him as odd because he had no problem letting others captain a ship while he hung out down below in his quarters without a care in the world.

It all came back to his crazy-ass uncle who ruined him for life.

It hadn't been until he met Booker that he could go up without internally having a close call with a panic attack.

As the plane leveled out, so did his emotions, but that didn't stop him from holding his harness with a death grip.

CHAPTER 5

Kirby jumped from the helicopter and scowled as she scanned the area. She couldn't believe her grant was being canceled. She should have known they would pull her considering what happened. They had explained they would start over with her replacement when things calmed down, but for now, they felt it best that they didn't send anyone else over. They made it clear she wasn't to return.

Too late.

Two military men stood guard where her vehicles should have been stored along with three local military police. She didn't like the fact that they were heavily armed. Her gorillas didn't care for weapons. They understood the destruction and devastation that they represented.

But it was the local government officials that

made her exceptionally nervous. While she'd always been on good terms with most of the local authorities, some viewed her as an interloper and would prefer she went away.

However, her mind went to the gorillas.

Tav—the silverback of the main group she'd been studying—tolerated her cameras. However, he once took one right out of her hands and stepped on it, crushing it. To this day, she would swear on her grandmother's grave that Tav smiled as he walked away.

One of the US servicemen strolled over to Wyatt. "I'm Petty Officer First Class Markus Waxman. Everyone calls me Waxman."

"Wyatt." He stretched out his hand. "Over there you've got Booker, Hunter, Xavier, Gunn, and this is Kirby. It was her team that was ambushed here two days ago."

"Sorry for your loss, ma'am." Waxman nodded. "My buddy there is Petty Officer Andrew Budder. We call him Budman."

"And who are the grumpy-looking guys over there?" Wyatt jerked his chin toward the path leading up the mountainside.

"Local police," Waxman said. "They don't speak much. Mostly grunt and balk at our presence because they are here to make sure we don't fuck anything up for them. But watch your step at the camp. While they knew you were coming, they aren't thrilled at the idea of you spending any time here. There's a bit of an issue between governments."

"I heard," Wyatt said.

"I don't follow." Kirby narrowed her eyes, glaring.

"We'll talk about that in a minute," Wyatt said. "Anything to report?"

"No, sir," Waxman said. "It's been quiet. We haven't seen anyone other than a few locals walking from one village to the next. No poachers, but I'm sure having locals and us here are helping to keep them away."

"Where are my vehicles?" Kirby asked.

"There was nothing here when we arrived. The local police might have taken them, or it could have been the poachers," Waxman said.

"Did you ask the local cops?" Wyatt asked.

"Their answers are vague and we don't seem to be on the need-to-know basis," Waxman said. "My CO has been on the horn with the Department of Defense, the government here, and anyone who will listen, but you know how that red tape works."

"I do," Wyatt said.

"What about my gorillas? Have you seen any of them?" Kirby asked with her pulse pounding between her temples. Her brain couldn't categorize the logistics of what Waxman had relayed regarding the deaths of her team members. She couldn't comprehend why there would be a problem. Innocent people were murdered. Both governments should want to get to the bottom of it, not argue over bureaucracy and jurisdiction. It didn't make much sense. Then again, the hoops she had to jump through to renew her work permit had been a nightmare. She almost had to leave the country because she accidentally forgot to initial one line.

"We've seen a grouping of gorillas not far from the basecamp. We've stayed clear. They are quite impressive and a little scary."

Kirby's heart swelled, but she knew deep down, some had to have been slaughtered. "How many did the poachers get?"

"There were five dead gorillas, ma'am." Waxman held her gaze. "We buried the bodies. We thought that would be the respectful thing to do."

"Yes. Thank you." She nodded. However, she would have liked to have seen which ones were murdered. "This might seem odd, but were any pictures taken of the dead animals?"

"Yes, ma'am." Waxman nodded. "One of the men up at basecamp will have them on his phone. He'll be more than happy to give them to you. However, there are four other local military police there as well. I believe the time you will be allowed to stay is limited."

"Why?" she asked.

"It's complicated," Waxman said. "The US ambassador is working on getting his people here."

"I wish someone had told us that." Wyatt raked a hand across the top of his head. "We would have been happy to provide transport."

Waxman chuckled. "No offense, but you're no longer with the military, sir, and the ambassador here is a stickler for the rules. He also views outfits like yours as…" Waxman glanced toward the sky. "…problematic."

"Of course he does." Wyatt shook his head. "How many men do you still have in the area?"

"Six," Waxman said. "The two of us here. Two at the camp. And two on the east side of the ridge. I would have preferred the west, but that's where the gorillas are and we don't want to be near them."

"That's probably a good idea," Wyatt said.

"Tell your men to stay low and quiet if they do come in contact with a gorilla, especially a silverback. And if one charges, don't run. Hold your ground." Kirby remembered the first time she'd been charged at and she seriously thought she was going to die.

"We were warned." Waxman nodded. "But I can't imagine that would be an easy thing to do."

"It's the only thing you can do, unless you want to be ripped apart like a turkey wishbone," Kirby said.

"You've got to be kidding me?" Wyatt stared at her with wide eyes.

"I'm dead serious. You run from a gorilla and you

just signed your death wish." Kirby patted Wyatt on the shoulder.

"You're afraid of cockroaches, but a five-hundred-pound gorilla doesn't make you flinch." Wyatt visibly shivered.

"If I did that, I'd be dead," she said. "We should start the hike up. I want to be able to see the gorillas before sundown."

Wyatt held up an earpiece. "We need to sync up our comms before we go."

"Not a problem." Waxman and Wyatt made their way across the open field to the helicopter.

She'd let them do their thing while she collected her thoughts and put her emotions in check. The overwhelming sensation of dread had engulfed her during the last ten minutes of the helicopter ride. The only survivor of her team had been Ben and he was barely hanging on. They wanted to transfer him to Germany, but he hadn't stabilized enough for the doctors to feel comfortable that he'd live through the flight there.

The guilt of not being with her team filled every fiber of her being. She should have died. Had she not been so selfish, maybe she would have been able to see the poachers coming. Or at least… who the fuck was she kidding. She couldn't have done anything and that was the worst part.

Tears scorched her cheeks.

"Hey." Wyatt rested his hand on her shoulder.

She jumped.

"Sorry," he whispered, wiping her tears away with his thumb. "If you're not up for this, I can have someone fly you to—"

"I have to do this."

"The military removed the bodies of your team," Wyatt said. "They're being taken back to the US."

"I'm glad. I don't think I could have seen that."

"I wouldn't want you to," Wyatt said. "But there's something else I need to tell you."

She cocked her head.

"Technically, we're here as your escorts and you're only here to collect a few personal items you left behind." He placed both hands on her shoulders, lowering his chin. "We have twenty-four hours to get in and get out."

"Excuse me? What about finding out who did this and stopping them?"

"Both governments just tied my hands."

She shrugged his hands off her body. "When? How?"

"I found out between getting off the small prop plane and into the choppers."

"And you thought you'd wait to tell me this now?"

"I hadn't planned on following that order," Wyatt said with a stern tone. "Stone gave me the go-ahead to stay as long as necessary, but the moment we landed and saw those guys with machine guns over there. Well, that's when we had to weigh our choices."

"Some of them have a decent understanding of English." She took him by the hand and led him further away from where the two local cops stood. "I need to get a good count of the gorillas and I can't do that in a day. Not to mention I have no idea what's left up there. It could take more than one trip down the mountainside."

"We get as much as we can." Wyatt ran his hand up and down her arm. "But staying here isn't going to do any good. The poachers or whoever did this won't come here with the military police standing guard. We need to think outside the box if we're going to find out who did this."

"I wish Hunter had better luck in the village when he went looking for a trophy and meat."

"People could have seen him with you, or maybe everyone is too scared with all the activity because of what happened. There's a lot of chatter about it."

Kirby couldn't argue that point. Wyatt and his team might not be wearing uniforms, but they screamed military. "Many of the villagers looked at me as if they'd seen a ghost."

"I noticed that too." Wyatt glanced over his shoulder. "Stone made it clear that we were to leave this location when we were told. But he didn't say we had to leave the Congo."

"What are you suggesting?"

"It depends on what we can learn about who's responsible for killing your team." He looped his arm around her waist. "Stone is looking into the poaching ring you crippled."

"You really believe this was revenge and they meant to kill me?"

"I do," Wyatt said. "Every other poaching had only been about the gorillas. They never attacked you or your people."

Her heart broke for every life lost. They had given up time with their families to help her with her research. Their work had been invaluable to her and she'd been grateful to have such a wonderful team. An insurmountable sense of culpability filled her soul.

She had no idea how she'd ever move past the pain that filled the center of her chest.

"That's not entirely true," she said. "There was one time where Tim—he was with me for about a year—tried to stop them and he was shot in the leg. He went home and never came back. I can't say as I blame him. It was scary because once he went down, the gorillas weren't sure if he was friend or foe and he got scratched up pretty good by one."

"But the poachers felt threatened. That wasn't the case this time. Your team—according to the report—was sitting around the table eating dinner. They didn't see or hear them coming. It was a total ambush." Wyatt scratched his head and crinkled his brow.

"You get that look when you think too hard."

"You mentioned that Ben was supposed to make the supply run back to the States, but the order was messed up and he denied making the mistake. It seems strange to me for that to happen on the same trip that your team ended up dead."

"I'm not following."

"Ben got away," Wyatt said.

"Barely. He was shot and nearly died. He still could."

"How long would he have been gone if he made the supply run?"

"He would have been in and out," Kirby said. "Six days tops. He would have flown in, checked the order, and brought it back, only staying two days to do personal things."

"What exactly is in that order? Don't you get all your food locally? And why is it necessary for you to go Stateside to get it?"

"Am I being interrogated?" Kirby asked.

"I'm just trying to understand a few things while my mind works overtime formulating a million and one scenarios."

"Sometimes I hate your genius brain," she muttered. "It's mostly medication, medical supplies, and things I can't get locally. We don't always fly over and get it ourselves, but I've found when I don't, things are missing. So, for the last three years, I've done it religiously and Ben and I've often… holy shit. I didn't think about this."

"What?" Wyatt asked.

"After I told Ben I was going instead of him, he made the comment that he'd been planning on staying in the States for a little longer than normal. I told him that I had meetings and if it wasn't all that important, I'd make it up to him, letting him go as soon as I got back. He agreed to that, saying he could reschedule his plans."

"Do you know what those plans were? Was he meeting someone? Family? A girlfriend? A buddy? Anyone we could contact?"

"I honestly have no idea. Ben's an odd duck. He's a great assistant. Organized. Effective and efficient. Hard worker. But we're not close, at least not on a personal level."

"How is that possible? There were only eight of you up here. It was impossible for me not to get close to my men. I had to. We were each other's lifeline." Wyatt waved his hand toward Booker and the rest of his team. "You lived here with him for three years. It's a remote place and they were all that you had. I'm sorry, but I find it hard to believe that you didn't know him on some intimate level."

"He was a private man. He didn't let anyone in and it wasn't for lack of trying by me or anyone else on my team." She resented the way Wyatt spoke to her, as if something was wrong with how she handled the people she worked with. She respected their right to privacy. They had a job to do. If they didn't want to get too personal with the people they worked with, that was their prerogative. "When we would sit around the campfire at night, he would join us and share in a beverage, but he never went deep."

"What can you tell me about him?"

In all the years Kirby had known Wyatt, she'd never seen him in work mode. Whenever she'd visited him, he was usually on leave. If he wasn't and he was at base, she never saw him in action. This was new territory. He'd always been an intense guy. She could see his drive in anything they did. He was super competitive in sports. Like when they'd go kayaking, he'd want to turn it into a race. He loved to push himself to the limit when he worked out and got frustrated when his injuries got in the way.

When he'd been forced out of the Navy because of the crash, he'd been lost with no direction as to what to do next. His whole world had come down on him like a ton of bricks. She worried he'd never find something that would light up his world again until Booker made the deal with the Brotherhood Protectors.

Wyatt's excitement at the opportunity had filled her heart with joy.

But right now, his rapid-fire questions grated on her last nerve.

"What exactly do you want to know?" She fiddled with her ponytail as she struggled to find the right response.

"Basic information about him as a person." Wyatt arched a brow.

She knew precisely where he was going with this line of questioning and she didn't appreciate it but understood it. "He was dedicated to my cause in the protection of mountain gorillas. There's no way he could have had anything to do with this, so don't even go there."

"Come on, Kirby. Think about it. He was the one who was supposed to be gone. Not you."

"Okay. But if that were true, why didn't he call it off? Why did he get shot?"

"Maybe he tried but couldn't reach the poachers. Maybe the organization responsible thought he sent you away; therefore, he betrayed them."

"I hate it when you fucking make sense," she mumbled. "But I don't believe it."

"I wouldn't want to either, but we need to consider it."

"Comms are all set up," Waxman yelled.

"We better get going." Hunter pointed toward the trail.

Wyatt placed a hand on her back. "We'll contact Stone and have him look into Ben's background. I'll also contact the hospital and see what belongings Ben had with him. Maybe the satphone can give us some answers. Or maybe he had another form of communication on him."

"There is no cell reception here. Only in the

village. If he had his phone, the only communication he could have had with anyone would have been the last time he went to town and we have a rule. One of the two of us has to be at camp at all times. If I'm gone, he can't leave."

"Rules are broken every day."

CHAPTER 6

Kirby stood over one of the gravesites of the murdered gorillas. Tears welled in her eyes as the images the Navy SEAL had shown her flashed in her mind.

Decapitated.

Hands and feet cut off.

Two of the larger ones were mutilated for their meat.

The sound of boots rustling through the leaves on the ground caught her attention.

She wiped her cheeks before turning.

"You okay?" Wyatt asked.

"No. I'm not." She rubbed her hands on her jeans. "How can you not believe this was about poachers after seeing the brutality of what those bastards did to these precious creatures?"

Wyatt inched closer, cupping the back of her

neck. His warm lips firmly pressed against her forehead in a loving kiss. "I'm certainly not saying they didn't want the gorillas. But I think that this was more opportunity than the main goal."

She jerked her head. "They butchered innocent animals."

"They did the same thing to your team." Wyatt dropped his hands to his sides. "They destroyed your camp. Took almost everything that was there. Your equipment. Supplies. Went through your cabin, breaking everything inside. Not to mention the message they left."

She shivered. She couldn't deny that seeing an image of herself pinned to the door with a circle and a line through it hadn't shaken her up. "We don't know what that meant."

"It's a clear sign that they want to kill you." Wyatt stuffed his hands in his pockets and scowled. "Stop trying to pretend that wasn't their intention and that they only cared about the damn gorillas. I know you love them and you've spent five years of your life living with them. Studying their community and how they live. I get you want to protect all endangered species. I love that about you. Your passion. It's one of the things that draws me to you. But someone wants you dead and now it's my job to protect you."

"It's not going to matter because the organization that controls my grant is going to pull me from here anyway. As a matter of fact, I'm not even supposed to be here. They are no longer responsible for me."

"I'm sorry that happened." He reached out and ran his thumb across her lower lip. "I'm here to protect you. So that's covered. But we are leaving tomorrow."

"I can't just pack up and go home with my tail between my legs. I owe it to my team—and the gorillas—to find out who did this and bring them to justice."

"I already told you we're not leaving the Congo. Not yet anyway."

"Where do you plan on having us go?" she asked. "For five years I've lived in this one spot. There are other areas I can take you where I know there are gorillas, but it takes time for me to establish trust with the animals."

"I'm not suggesting we go sit and wait to be ambushed. My team is going through the camp, looking for clues. Whoever did this has to know you're back. We need to draw them out. What I don't like is doing it out here where I don't know the lay of the land and they have the upper hand." He glanced over his shoulder.

Hunter and Xavier appeared through the thick brush.

"The US ambassador is here," Xavier said. "He's got an entire entourage with him. Ten people in all. One is a DEA agent."

Wyatt rubbed the side of his scruffy cheek. "That's an interesting combo."

"He also brought one cameraman and newsperson," Hunter said.

"Shit. I forgot to call my parents," Kirby muttered. "They are going to flip out."

"It made headlines in the States yesterday." Wyatt squeezed her shoulder. "Everyone will know you're alive soon enough."

She let out a sigh. "Was it reported that I was in Montana?"

"No," Hunter said. "The report indicated that it was believed you'd flown to DC for medical supplies."

"Wonderful. So, now my folks will be freaking out as to why I haven't rushed home. They will dislike you even more now if they think I'm with you."

"I didn't realize they had feelings about me one way or the other. Hell, I'm kind of shocked they even know about me." He arched a brow.

She shrugged. "I had to tell them something when I'm in the States for ten days and only with them for four."

"The ambassador would like to speak with her and the news crew wants to interview her," Xavier said.

"Absolutely not." Wyatt shook his head.

"And why not? Didn't you just say you wanted to draw out the bastards who killed my team?" she said.

"Yeah, by being seen in a nearby village. Not flashed all over the globe in an interview. We need people to be willing to talk with us and doing an interview with the media could work against you." Wyatt's tone came off a little too harsh for her liking and she certainly didn't agree.

"Most locals love me. They see me as their friend. I help preserve their land," she said.

"And stand in the way of their progress." Wyatt held up his hand. "The only way I'll agree to an interview with the press is if I can see the questions first. If you agree to allow me to end the interview if they go off script. And they are focused on this being about the poaching. I want to spin this exactly the way you keep trying to push it on me. I don't want the assholes to think we know this is solely a revenge killing."

She narrowed her stare. "That's a huge contradiction to what you were saying a few minutes ago."

"No. It's not. I still believe someone is out to get you—and only you—but there's no reason to put that out there. Let them believe we think it's all about the gorillas."

"Wyatt's right," Hunter said. "The bastards will take it as a win. That we're on the stupid side and they can come at you and we'll be ready."

"That doesn't make me feel better," she said under her breath.

"You've got to trust that we know what we're

doing." Wyatt wrapped his arm around her waist. "Come on. Let's go chat with the ambassador and his entourage."

∼

Wyatt sat on a log and twiddled a stick, staring at Kirby while she prepared for the interview.

"How ya doing?" Booker stepped over the stump, picked up a stick, and plopped his ass on the log. "Because you look like you swallowed a lemon."

"I'm not thrilled with this idea."

"I can tell," Booker said.

"Were you able to reach Callie on the satphone?"

"I did and she doesn't know Agent Ridley from the DEA personally, but said he's got a stellar reputation, although he's known for occasionally going rogue. Nothing that we wouldn't have done, but it's gotten him in hot water once or twice. However, she believes, and I concur, if he's here, there's more to this poaching ring than our government is letting on."

"That's not news."

"Callie will poke around. Call a few contacts. Pull in a few favors and see what she can find out about Ridley and what he's up to."

"What about the group that's in prison?"

"Amari Okoro and seven of his crew are behind bars here in Africa. Stone learned the local government believes he's part of a bigger ring, but he couldn't get much on what they are doing about it, if anything."

"So, perhaps not the main man." Wyatt had already known that piece of information. He'd followed the story as it unfolded, but unfortunately, the African government could be tight-lipped about some of it.

"That I don't know. These groups often compete with each other and from what Callie has found out and what Kirby has stated, they will kill each other over gorillas."

"Or form bigger coalitions."

"If the DEA is here, it could be running guns or drugs and that's an entirely new game. One that goes way beyond the sale of gorilla trophies," Booker said.

"Makes me wonder what her assistant could have gotten himself into."

"Exactly."

"I bet he screwed up that shipment on purpose because he was going to smuggle something into or out of Africa." Wyatt tossed his stick to the ground. "That would have pissed off whoever he was working with."

"That means it could have been him they were after."

"I thought of that, but why threaten Kirby then," Wyatt said. "She stood in their way, especially if they ever approached her to be part of their operation."

Booker pursed his lips. "You don't think she'd keep that juicy little nugget from you, do you?"

"I'd like to believe she would have told me. That would have infuriated her and knowing her the way I do, she would have brought it to someone's attention. However, she's hyper focused on the gorillas and poaching. She has been since she got here." Wyatt stood, stretching out his back. "She wasn't here for more than a month the first time she experienced it. Since then, she's made it her mission to stop them. It's been as important to her as studying the gorillas' community and family life."

"She is quite passionate about her work." Booker rose. "If someone had asked her to do something illegal, I can't imagine she would have kept quiet. She's not the type."

Wyatt nodded. "But she has blind spots. She trusts those who work for her explicitly, which she needs to. However, she can't see what's right in front of her when push comes to shove."

"Like the fact she's in love with you too." Booker smiled that stupid grin he had when he thought he had all the answers.

"Shut up about that. This isn't the time or place."

"It's the perfect time." Booker slapped him on the back. "It's so obvious it's almost painful to watch. The two of you have been doing this stupid dance with each other for too long. I don't know what the hell you're afraid of. You're in a relationship whether you've defined it or not. You might as well say the words and move on."

"It's complicated."

"Why? Because she was living here and you were deployed all over the globe? Or because you chose to make it that way and keep your fucking feelings to yourself?" Booker let out an exasperated sigh. "You're going to ruin the best thing outside of me that has ever happened to you if you don't tell her you love her."

Wyatt glanced in Kirby's direction.

She'd taken her hair and braided it over her shoulder. She wore a black tank top and jeans. She looked up, smiled, and waved.

His heart dropped to his toes.

Loving her was the easy part.

But putting it all out there after seven years of pretending it was something he could take or leave was utterly terrifying. It was as if he were saying it was all or nothing. The last thing he wanted was to let her go.

"Those words aren't something you blurt out randomly. The timing has to be perfect," Wyatt said.

Booker burst out laughing. "If you're waiting for that, you'll be waiting for hell to freeze over." He cleared his throat. "You'll have her cabin to yourself tonight. No time like the present."

"No fucking way. The ambassador is staying the night because it will be too dark to head back down. I also get the impression he wants to keep an eye on us, which gives me a bad feeling."

"You're deflecting. What the hell does he have to do with your love life? Stop putting this off. Trust me."

"I'll see how the evening goes." Wyatt hoped that would end the conversation.

"You're a fool if you don't," Booker said.

"Looks like they're ready for the interview." Wyatt stuffed his hands in his pockets and strolled across the campground. Sally Weidmore, a reporter from CNN whom he'd had a nice little chat with, had promised to keep the discussion focused on the poaching, but she had made it clear that for obvious reasons, she needed to include the deaths of the American citizens. Wyatt had no problem with that. His only concern had been the fact that she had been tipped off that there was more to this story than the gorillas.

The DEA agent had denied his presence had anything to do with guns or drugs. That he'd come as a personal favor to the ambassador simply because he'd been in the area on another matter, but couldn't —or wouldn't—go into the details.

Bullshit.

He was there because he knew something and he wasn't telling Wyatt or his team shit. Something that needed to change.

CHAPTER 7

Kirby handed the mic to Sally. "Thank you so much for doing this."

"I'm so sorry about what happened to your team and to the gorillas," Sally said. "It's a tragedy what goes on here."

"Unfortunately, it's been going on forever. Many believe it's an internal problem. But the foreigners who come into this country drive the sale of gorilla trophies, not the locals."

"I truly appreciated your honesty in the interview. I believe it will bring a ton of awareness to the situation here and help the mountain gorilla continue to thrive."

"Sadly, my time here is over. I didn't mention this on camera, but I'm not supposed to be here. Once the organization that funds me found out I was Stateside when it happened, they ordered me not to return, but I was already here."

"So, this interview could get you in trouble?"

Kirby shrugged. "The grant's already been pulled. It was scheduled to end in six months. They just moved it up. All this means is they aren't responsible if anything happens to me. I have no safety net, so to speak."

Sally lifted her chin. "You have that handsome devil and his team to protect you."

Kirby glanced over her shoulder. Her pulse increased. Wyatt was in a deep, intense conversation with Agent Ridley. Wyatt had a wide stance, his arms folded, and his chest puffed out. It was a powerful and intimidating image. She couldn't imagine what put Wyatt into that kind of mode. Last time she'd seen that was when he nearly got into a brawl with a couple of yahoos in a bar who were harassing a young woman.

"Is he your boyfriend?" Sally stuffed the mic and some other things into a packsack.

This wasn't the first time someone had asked Kirby that question. Depending on the situation, she gave different answers. She never cared what people thought of her arrangement with Wyatt. It had been working for them for years. He'd been busy with his career as a SEAL and she with her gorillas. They had goals and being committed to a relationship would only muck things up for both of them.

However, ever since the crash that forced Wyatt into an early retirement from the military, a shift in her emotions left her wanting more and that was something she'd been unprepared to deal with, so she chose to put those feelings in a tiny box in the corner of her heart. Only, she couldn't ignore them anymore.

"I'm not exactly sure," she admitted.

Sally blinked. "The reporter in me wants to know more." She set her pack on the ground. "The woman in me is curious why you're keeping him at arm's length when it's clear he cares a great deal about you."

Kirby had few girlfriends. There had been two women on her team and while she loved them dearly, she struggled to bond with them on a more personal level. It wasn't the ladies that was the problem.

It was Kirby.

She didn't trust most of the female population. The first woman her father had an affair with had been her seventh grade science teacher. What made that so horrible was that Ms. Horaway had been her favorite teacher and Ms. Horaway had made it perfectly clear that Kirby was her star pupil. The whole thing had crushed Kirby. She'd been too young to process the information and had no one to turn to for advice.

When the affair ended, she thought she could forget all about it, but then her father decided it was time to move on to her soccer coach and it didn't end there.

At the ripe old age of sixteen, Kirby brought the information to her mother, believing she was doing the right thing. What happened next defined the way Kirby approached relationships, or the lack of them. It floored her that her mom had known about each affair and responded with: *sometimes men have to do these things. He's a good father and a good provider. That's what matters.*

Kirby will always remember those words.

"It's complicated."

"How?" Sally asked. "Is there something wrong with him?"

"God, no," Kirby said. "He's one of the good guys. Our lives are just so separate and different. It makes it difficult to be in a full-time relationship."

"But do you love him?"

Now that was a question no one had ever asked. Her cheeks heated. Her blood turned hot. Every muscle burned with a desire that wasn't purely physical.

"Wow," Sally said. "You're in love with him but can't even admit it to yourself."

"Like I said, it's complicated."

"Love always is." Sally squeezed her forearm. "My husband was a Green Beret. When we met, I was starting out in my career and he was at West Point. We probably spent more time apart those first ten years than we did together. Sometimes we still do even though he's now in the reserves, and I'm still obviously doing my thing. But the one thing I do know is that when it's true love, it does conquer all."

She swallowed. She'd often wondered if her father actually loved her mother and vice versa. She couldn't imagine why they stayed together for forty years. To the outside world, they appeared happy. Hell, even to her, they didn't seem as though there were problems in their marriage. They always had family dinners that consisted of everyone discussing their day. They went out to dinner and did all the things other married couples did, except they had absolutely nothing in common. Her mom volunteered in the neighborhood and was active in the church. Two things her dad wanted nothing to do with. Her father had his golf and poker, which he did as if it were his religion.

If she were being honest with herself, her parents put on a show for the outside world—and their daughter—but in reality, they might as well have lived separate lives. Kirby left as soon as she graduated high school and didn't return except for long weekends to visit.

"Can I ask you a crazy question that might be incredibly off-putting and totally inappropriate?"

Sally laughed. "I bet you're going to ask if either of us ever stepped out on our marriage."

"I'm sorry. I know that's a horrible thing to ask a stranger."

"Nah. It's something that most people assume. I've had men hit on me, believing that I'd be willing because my husband is gone and I must be lonely. My husband has had women throw themselves at him, assuming he needs a warm body because I'm not around. And don't get me going on some of my so-called friends telling me why they believe Josh must be cheating. It's crazy. But I can assure you that neither one of us has ever. It takes work. A lot of communication. And a level of commitment and dedication to the relationship. It's not just about love. That's the foundation. But it's more about building a life together. Supporting each other and whatever the other person wants. He never once asked me to stop pursuing my dreams and I encouraged him to follow his."

Kirby's mind drifted to her childhood. Memories of the dinner table and her mom mentioning going back to school and her father giving her a dozen reasons why she couldn't.

They didn't have the money.

Her responsibility was raising Kirby and taking care of him.

Anger flared in her belly.

While she loved her dad, the older she got, the more she realized how emotionally controlling he'd been of her mom.

And how he'd tried to do it with her, which was why she avoided home and introducing Wyatt to the family.

Wyatt was the polar opposite of her dad.

She loved him with her entire soul. Wyatt had sent her a toy gorilla when she'd received her grant. It wasn't a huge gesture, but in the card he told her how proud he'd been.

Her father had been mortified and tried to talk her out of going.

Wyatt had always supported her, even when he worried about her safety.

"Are you concerned about him being a cheater?" Sally asked.

"No," Kirby admitted. "In all the years I've known him, whenever we have seen someone else, we've been truthful about it. Honestly, that has only happened twice."

"So, he is your boyfriend."

"We've never defined what we are, except when I get back to the States, I see him." It felt damn fucking good to talk to someone other than herself about Wyatt. The only other person she'd could see herself having this conversation with would be Callie, but they were never alone to do it. "I haven't been with anyone other than him in three years. He hasn't been with anyone else either. But we still keep it casual. We have great sex. Great conversation, although nothing too deep. He hasn't met my family.

I haven't met his. We've never talked about a future together."

"No time like the present."

Kirby scoffed. "I don't think this would be the right time."

"Ha. The first time my husband told me he loved me was when I showed up for a story where he was deployed and bullets were flying. He proposed when I was on assignment in the Middle East," Sally said. "You're not changing the dynamics because you're already in a relationship. All you're doing is solidifying your feelings and ensuring you're on the same page. If you don't do it, things will get even more complicated and you could lose the man you love. I don't think you want to do that." She looped her arm around Kirby's waist and gave her a little shove. "Looks like they're done with their conversation. Go get your man."

⁂

"Stop lying to me." Wyatt folded his arms across his chest and widened his stance. "I know there's more to your visit than a favor to the ambassador."

"Even if that were the case, I couldn't tell you." Agent Ridley stuffed his hands in his pockets and dared to smile.

"My job is to protect Kirby and I can't do that unless I know what is going on."

"She's not even supposed to be here," Ridley said. "The ambassador wasn't thrilled about her presence, nor did he appreciate the camera crew. He only allowed it because Americans died and he doesn't want to create more hostility between the two countries. But he's worried the coverage will get out of hand."

"I can't say I enjoyed that either, but Sally handled it well, leaving it at the gorillas, which I'm sure you also had a hand in." Wyatt arched a brow. "We're on the same team here. We should work together, not opposing each other in our efforts."

"You're a protection detail. Not military anymore. That ties my hands."

"That's bullshit." It really wasn't and Wyatt knew it, but he would push as hard as he could. "I've worked with organizations like the Brotherhood Protectors as a SEAL. My men and I are good at our jobs. Use us."

Ridley threaded his fingers through his hair. "I can't."

"Give me one good reason why not."

"Because part of my job is to get you to leave." Ridley shifted his gaze in the direction of the ambassador. "While I needed Sally to keep this to poaching for the integrity of my investigation, the ambassador has other reasons and I'm walking a fine line here."

That statement alone was telling. "The United States appointed the ambassador. He's here to represent our interests. What the hell kind of game is he playing?"

"I'm not exactly sure," Ridley whispered. "But I believe it's a dangerous one."

Wyatt cocked his head. "You need to explain."

"I could lose my job if I do." Ridley jerked his chin and took five steps further away from the crowd.

Wyatt followed. "I have no intention of interfering with your investigation. But Kirby needs answers and I think she deserves them."

"I did a little research about you and your men before climbing up this mountain. You have a glowing service record. I couldn't find one negative thing about you, so I need your word that you won't say anything to Kirby. If you can't make that promise, this conversation ends here."

"I need to be able to inform my men." Wyatt's stomach pitched. Keeping shit from Kirby wouldn't go over well when she found out, but he needed the intel. He'd deal with the fallout later.

"I can live with that." Ridley nodded. "The ambassador is part of the reason why I'm here."

"No shit. That can't be good."

"It's not," Ridley said. "We believe he's helping a man named Kofi Igwe smuggle guns and drugs in and out of Africa. For two years we've been investigating this and it led us right to your girlfriend."

"Kirby? She's not involved in anything like that."

"The problem is that all roads lead to her. Or at least her supply chain."

"Impossible." Wyatt crossed his arms and puffed out his chest. "You're mistaken."

"Maybe about her, but not about some of the things I've learned," Ridley said. "But I don't have all the pieces."

"What do you have?"

"Ten months ago, we busted some of Kofi's men with guns from the US. We traced the source back in the States but are struggling with the how. We know there is an exchange between drugs, guns, and gorillas. The worst part is that local government officials and our ambassador are involved."

"Fuck me," Wyatt muttered. "Ben."

"Kirby's assistant?" Ridley asked. "He was nearly killed in the shootout."

"To make a long story short, Ben was supposed to make the medical supply run Stateside. Kirby made a last-minute change. When she got to DC, the order was all fucked up. Since that happened, I wondered if Ben did that on purpose, but I didn't know why. If he's part of this ring, it makes sense he'd cancel if that was supposed to be a different kind of shipment."

"It sure does, but why would they try to kill him?"

"I think they were after her for shutting down a poaching ring five months ago," Wyatt said. "She put a man by the name of—"

"Omari Okra." Ridley sighed. "We've looked for the

connection between him and Kofi and we can't find one. Two totally different bad guys with different agendas. Okra was strictly a poacher. Kofi is more into guns and drugs. Poaching is more of a game. He likes to hunt for fun and sell to the highest foreign bidder. You have to think bigger than Okra who sold in the village streets to anyone. Kofi deals only with those who are willing to pay top dollar and come to him first. He considers himself a dealer of fine arts when it comes to the gorilla. He hunts silverbacks more than anything."

"That doesn't mean the two men haven't struck up a friendship to achieve a common goal to get rid of Kirby."

Ridley lowered his chin. "I looked into that and Okra has not been contacted by Kofi or any known affiliate of Okra."

"But I'm sure the ambassador or other officials have." Wyatt arched a brow. "That's your connection."

"Unfortunately, that's true. But I have no proof. Hence, I'm the ambassador's new best friend."

"What does Sally know about any of this?" Wyatt asked.

"Nothing, except she's not stupid. For now, my bosses and the government are allowing her exposé on the gorillas, but we're doing our best to keep what we know about everything else under wraps, and I need you to do the same."

"I can do that. However, let's not tie each other's

hands. I'll give you anything I find out, if you do me the same favor."

"Within reason." Ridley stretched out his hand. "Don't make me regret this."

"You have my word." Wyatt stood there as he watched Ridley stroll toward his tent.

"That looked intense." Kirby appeared at his side. "Anything I should be aware of?"

"Yeah." He looped a protective arm around her body. "But you're not going to like the fact I'm not going to tell you right now."

She glanced up and glared. "You can't do that to me."

"I have to." He kissed her temple. "At least for right now. I'll fill you in when we leave tomorrow. For now, please keep any theory my team has told you to yourself. Don't say anything to the ambassador or even to Ridley."

"Why not?"

"Because I don't know who we can trust."

She paused midstep. "I thought you said Callie gave Ridley the thumbs-up."

"She said he has a stellar record, but that doesn't mean I trust him. I still don't want you to talk to him about shit. He needs to believe I'm keeping you in the dark."

"Fucking men. You're all a pain in the ass."

He chuckled. "I'll try really hard not to be that

guy, but until we get off this mountain, you're just going to have to trust that I've got your back."

She palmed his cheek.

Staring into her deep blue-green eyes, his heart dropped to his knees. It felt as though he'd been sucker punched.

"You're the only one I do trust. Well, outside of Booker."

"I knew it. You have a crush on him."

"I wouldn't kick him out of bed." She leaned in and kissed his lips. "I don't think you would either."

"Oh, hell yes, I would. He can't kiss to save his sorry ass."

"I don't know about that. I've seen the two of you in a lip-lock and it looked to me like you were into it."

"Gross." He gave her a hip check. "Come on. Let's go to bed. It's late and I know you want to go see your gorillas in the morning and say goodbye before we head down the mountain." His pulse beat so fast he thought his heart was going to explode. There was no other woman in the world who could fit into his life the way Kirby did.

Booker was right.

It was time to shit or get off the pot.

CHAPTER 8

Kirby stood in the center of her cabin. Not much had been salvaged from the poacher's destruction. Her makeshift dresser had been turned into kindling. Her clothes had been ripped to shreds. All her notebooks and paperwork had been torn and tossed about.

Wyatt had done his best to clean up the mess. A pile of what couldn't be saved was in the corner and what he'd been able to piece together of her work had been stacked on the desk he'd hammered back into one piece.

"We're going to have to sleep on the floor." Wyatt waved his hand over the sleeping bags he'd zipped together. "The mattress was destroyed."

"The local police wouldn't give me any information on their investigation." She shimmied out of her jeans and found a pair of sweatpants in her knapsack.

"They didn't tell me much either."

"What did you learn from Ridley?"

Wyatt raised his finger to his lips. "Not here. I can't risk someone could hear us," he whispered. "It's turning into a delicate situation requiring a unique approach. I will have to rethink how we go about this because I'm not sure being in this country is the way to do it."

"I'm not sure I understand."

"Now is not the time to discuss this." Wyatt climbed into the sleeping bag, patting the spot next to him. "We need to get some sleep. I want to be out of here by two at the latest. I know that doesn't give you much time, but we should be in the village by dinner to find a place to stay for the night. Booker and I need to devise a plan with the rest of the team. I must also call Stone to ensure he understands my thinking."

She snuggled in next to the only man—only person—who had been a constant in her life for seven years. To her knowledge, Wyatt had never lied to her about anything. Not even the few times when he'd dated other women. She acted as if it didn't matter, but she'd been devastated. She reacted by finding someone else to wrap her arms around. However, they weren't Wyatt.

He never pressured her to come home or give up her life's dream. All he ever did was support and encourage.

"I'd like to comprehend too." She rested her head on his strong shoulder.

"You will. I promise." He kissed her temple. "There are a lot of things I want to tell you, but I'm not sure how to express them."

She tilted her head, catching his gaze. "Like what?"

He rolled to his side, holding her in his loving arms. There was nothing about Wyatt she didn't appreciate. There hadn't been a time he hadn't been there for her when she'd reached out. It might have taken him a few hours or even a day to respond, depending on where in the world or what time zone he'd been in, but he always let her know he was there, willing and able to listen. He would often message her, offering support and advice. She never felt judged and even the smallest of problems he wouldn't dare belittle.

"You've been in my life for a long time." He tucked her hair behind her ear. His dark eyes bore deep into her soul. "We might not have spent that much time together over the years, but I think about you every day we're not together."

"I think about you too." Her heart lurched to her throat.

"I've been wondering what will happen next, especially now that your grant is up." He fanned his thumb across her cheek. "Are you going to come back to the States?"

"I have no idea," she admitted. "It wasn't supposed to happen for another six months. I was planning on researching possible new grants to study the communities of a different species."

"I remember when you got the grant for the gorillas; it started as a two-year deal."

She let out a short, dry chuckle. "I fell in love with those beasts, and then the work I did with stopping the poachers took on a life of its own. Not to mention the book deal. But now that's done, so it's time to move on."

"But to what?" His finger danced up and down her arm, sending a fire across her belly, making it difficult to think straight.

"I'm not sure. My passion has always been endangered creatures and animals that have strong family and community bonds. Studying those things is where I need to be. My original thought was to take some time off and go to Utah. My parents have been putting a shit ton of pressure on me to go home. They complain I haven't been there for over a week at a time since graduating high school."

"There's a reason you don't go back for more than a few days." He arched a brow.

Few people in her circle knew about her dad. She'd told Wyatt about the situation one night after coming back from visiting her folks. She'd seen a text from one of her father's latest conquests and it sent her over the edge. When she showed up at Wyatt's, she'd lost her shit and got drunk spilling the entire sordid tale.

Once again, Wyatt listened without trying to make her feel better or make excuses for either of her parents' behavior. He didn't judge her for overindulging in adult beverages, though he did try to stop her, reminding her how she would regret it in the morning.

Which she did.

However, he didn't demand she never speak of it again, like her folks. He also didn't suggest she confront her father or her mom.

He was just there like a good boyfriend, even though he wasn't anything other than a friend with benefits.

"I can't avoid them for the rest of my life." She let out a long breath. "They both know that I'm well aware of my dad's extracurricular activities. They have to know it's why I prefer to be elsewhere."

"I was a little surprised you told them about me. Maybe they believe you enjoy spending time wherever I am." He winked.

She laughed. "My dad doesn't like you."

Wyatt jerked his head back. "He doesn't even know me."

"That's part of the reason he doesn't care for you and the other reason is he thinks you're a coward for never coming to Utah with me. He believes a real man would join his woman—his words not mine—while she visited her family."

"What the hell have you told them?" Both of Wyatt's brows shot up.

"Not much actually, but when they know I'm in the States for two weeks and only at their place for half that, I did have to give them a name and place."

"You could have lied," Wyatt said. "Now when I do meet them, I'm really going to have to turn on the charm."

She rested her chin on the center of his chest and stared at his beautiful face. Since he'd left the military, he'd let his facial hair grow. It wasn't a full beard and mustache, but it was enough and it was sexy as hell. His hair was a little longer than regulation but still short. However, now she could run her fingers through it, and she did as often as she could. "My mom will fall in love with you in an instant, but she'll assume you're a cheater."

"That makes me sad. Not because she'll think that about me, but for her."

"I know." Kirby nodded. "I have no idea how my dad will respond. I haven't brought a boyfriend home since college and he still believes I'm the one who screwed up that relationship."

"First off, that's not true, and secondly, is that what I am? A boyfriend?"

Her heart got stuck halfway between her throat and where it belonged. It thumped uncomfortably, making it difficult to swallow. "We've been dancing around this topic for a long time, haven't we?"

"It was a direct question, not a slow waltz."

"But we do the waltz so well."

"Don't you think it's time to change the song?" He lifted her chin, brushing his mouth over her lips. "I care about you and there isn't anyone else I'd rather be with. Please come to West Yellowstone and spend a few months there. We need to find out what we are to each other because I believe we have something special."

"I care about you too." She wanted desperately to tell him she loved him but couldn't form the words. Fear had a death grip on her heart. She knew he wasn't her father. Or Edwin who had destroyed her faith in men altogether. She'd given Edwin her soul and he'd stomped on it by sleeping with her roommate, among other things. It was as if she were living her parents' life and that was a world she wanted nothing to do with. Wyatt had offered her the freedom to be with someone who asked nothing of her, including a commitment.

But now she wanted more. Needed more.

However, she didn't know how to ask for it.

"So, what's stopping you giving us a chance? Because we've been in a relationship for the last few years whether we've defined it or not."

Her lips parted, but not a single word rolled off her tongue. He hadn't declared love, but he'd put something out there that required a response. This was almost everything she wanted and yet, she couldn't bring herself to unlock the emotions. They had been stored so deep she could barely find them.

"Kirby, I can't imagine what life would look like without you in it and honestly, I don't want to find out."

"What if my work takes me out of the country again?"

"We'd figure that out. But didn't you once tell me that wolves fascinated you? That you'd always wanted to study them?" he asked. "There are wolf sanctuaries all over Yellowstone. Not to mention the protection the park offers them. I know a few people who are involved and have spoken to—"

"You've discussed me working there without talking to me first?" She jumped to her knees. "Why would you do that? I can't stand shit like that and you know it." When she'd blurted out all the crap about her family, she'd also gone into all the bullshit she'd dealt with during her relationship with Edwin. Not just his cheating, though that was bad enough. But it was his controlling and manipulations that had driven her crazy. He didn't want her to go into her chosen profession. The idea of her traveling to foreign countries didn't fit into *his* plan and he constantly tried to force her to change her goals.

She nearly did that when she found out she was pregnant, but then she caught him in bed with her roommate. There was no way in hell she'd have a child with a man like that. She wouldn't raise a kid in the same world she had to experience her entire life. Having an abortion haunted to her to this day. She knew she'd made the right decision, but that didn't erase the guilt and shame that went with the choice.

Wyatt raised his hands. "All I did was ask a few questions and snag a brochure. I didn't commit you to anything. I was going to give it to you as something to consider. I wouldn't speak for you or assume it was something you should do. I want to be with you and that's hard when we're only together a couple of weeks here and there."

"Why do you always have to be so sweet and good at this?" She eased back into his arms. "You make it impossible to stay mad at you."

"Does that mean you'll consider coming to West Yellowstone for a bit?"

"It's hard to answer that while we're in the middle of all this shit."

"That's fair. However, it could be weeks, even months before we have all the answers and this is put to bed. It will not be safe for you to be in this country. Being with me is the safest place."

"You really think it will take that long?"

"My job was to come here and investigate and protect you. Unfortunately, both governments are taking away my abilities to find answers." He pressed his finger over her lips. "We'll stay in-country for a few days and see what we can find. I'm in no way suggesting I've given up. I want you to understand that forces are working against me, which is not a good position for me and my team. While we're on this mountain, I can't tell you anything else. You just have to trust me."

"I can do that." She rested her hand on the center of his chest. "Your heart is beating a mile a minute." For the most part, Wyatt was one of the calmest people she knew. Of course, she didn't spend time with him on the job. She knew from Booker he could be serious, a little high-strung, but he tended to be as cool as cucumber as well while in the field. So, it seemed odd that his pulse would be raging in this moment.

"That's because I'm nervous as fuck."

"Because of the things you can't tell me?"

"No," he whispered. "Because of what I want to tell you, but I'm terrified it will scare you so badly, you'll kick me out of this sleeping bag."

"Up until today, I wouldn't have believed you were afraid of anything. But then I watched you get in that prop plane, and I'm sorry, but I wanted to laugh my ass off."

"Not fucking funny." He grumbled. "And neither is this."

"Okay, but you won't know if it will freak me out if you don't tell me what's got your pulse raging out of control and is now sending mine to the moon."

She held her breath, waiting for him to speak his peace. She couldn't imagine what bothered him so badly. Whatever it was, she hoped it wouldn't piss her off.

∼

WYATT STARED AT THE CEILING. The light from the tiny battery-powered lamp glowed in the dark. He rested his head on one hand and kept the other around Kirby. He'd told her he cared but had successfully avoided his true feelings thanks to a heavy dose of fear.

He could admit that he'd never loved any other woman the way he loved Kirby. He'd had other relationships before her and he'd thought he'd been in love when he'd attended the Naval Academy. However, when they broke up, he hadn't been heartbroken. It had been easy enough for him to move on.

But there was no way in hell he'd ever be able to get over Kirby. His heart would forever belong to her and that was a fact he'd accepted.

Telling her was something he had to do. If he didn't, there would be no point in her coming to Yellowstone, especially if she didn't feel the same way or want to explore if her feelings could develop into something more. He owed it to both of them to let the emotions out.

"You're starting to scare me," Kirby said. "Is there something wrong?"

"No." He turned, palming her cheek, staring into her sweet blue-green eyes. He could get lost in those precious orbs. Her passion filtered through them like a portal into her soul. "I've never wanted to pressure you into making us a thing. I've enjoyed our *arrangement* for years just as much as you have. It's worked for us because of our careers and who we are as people. But a lot has changed in the last two years."

"If you didn't ask me to come to Yellowstone, I'd think you didn't want me around anymore," she said. "You're sending me mixed messages and now I'm confused."

He leaned in and brought her mouth to his, kissing her hard. "I haven't said this to a woman in years. The last time it left my lips was when I was thirty and I don't think I meant it."

"Oh my God. Whatever it is, say it because I'm creating different scenarios, and most of them aren't good. The one that isn't bad, I'm… I'm…" Her words trailed off and she closed her eyes. "I'm listening."

"Look at me," he said.

She blinked. "I don't think I'm ready for this."

"Okay." He pressed his lips against her forehead. "Get some sleep." He wasn't going to press his luck. Not tonight. They had forged new ground and she knew he cared. That was enough for now.

"Oh no." She poked his chest. "We came this far. I want to hear it."

"Hear what?"

"The words. Say them." She pulled back the sleeping bag and straddled him, leaning over him with her long hair flowing over her shoulders, covering part of his body.

He brushed it from her face. "You first."

"You brought this up."

"I'm a gentleman. Ladies should go first." He smiled.

She narrowed her eyes. "Age before beauty."

"I'm exactly one month older than you." He growled. "On one condition."

"What's that?"

"You take off that shirt and sports bra."

She cocked her head. "After you say it."

"You drive a hard bargain." He sucked in a deep breath, letting it out slowly. He felt as though his entire future dangled on how three words landed in her ears. She might know what he wanted to say. She might even feel it too. But that didn't mean she was going to say it back, which frightened him for different reasons.

Kirby wasn't the kind of woman who wore her emotions on her sleeve when it came to people. Animals yes, but not humans.

She wanted to be loved by her family. Appreciated for the woman she'd become, but her parents didn't value her or her work. They were too wrapped up in putting on a show for the community. It was important to them for their friends to see them as something they weren't. They lived a lie and expected their daughter to do the same thing.

Only she couldn't.

So she chose to leave.

That decision, however, also forced her to live in isolation, cutting herself off from close relationships. Well, that actually had a lot to do with her asshole ex-boyfriend. He'd been a real piece of work and when Wyatt had heard that story, he wanted to find that man and wring his neck.

He reached out, tracing his thumb across her lower lip. "Somehow in the last couple of years, I've fallen in love with you, Kirby Carrington."

She lifted her shirt over her head and tossed it across the room. Then came the bra, exposing her perfect round breasts.

His ability to think flew out the window.

But he wanted the words too. Needed them. He'd be lost forever without them.

He wouldn't force her to repeat them if she didn't feel the same way, but he had to know one way or the other.

She leaned closer, taking his mouth in a slow, tender kiss, letting it linger and build.

Breaking it off, he held her chin with the palm of his hand. "Kirby," he said with a shallow breath.

"Would it be too much to ask to know how you feel about what I just declared?"

She bit his lower lip.

"Ouch. What did you do that for?"

"I was making sure this was real."

"Shouldn't you be pinching yourself?"

She pressed her hands on his shoulders. Her gaze was as intense as a wildfire. "You know my history so you understand why I've always wanted to keep things casual."

"Is that what you still want?"

"We moved past that a long time ago." She threaded her fingers through his hair. "I've been so afraid of losing you that I thought changing anything about our arrangement would end it."

"That doesn't tell me how you feel."

"Like you, those three little words don't come easy," she said. "I've watched too many people in my life toss them around and not really mean them."

"I'm not your father or your ex."

"I know," she whispered. "And I do love you. I'm afraid that things will change now that we're defining this and saying it."

His heart swelled. She loved him and was willing to risk the words. He knew how hard it had been for her to admit it. They were similar that way. "That happened without us thinking about it." He pulled her closer. "There are no guarantees in life and we don't know where this will take us. The only promise

I can make you is that I won't lie to you. I won't cheat on you. And I will always do my best to support and be there for you."

"Sometimes I worry you are too good to be true."

He laughed. "I'm sure when we have more than a few days to spend together, you'll find all sorts of things to complain about. Trust me, I have faults."

"Name one."

"Alright." He squeezed her ass. "I have no desire to keep talking. I'm too horny."

"I don't see that as a fault." She rolled her hips, putting pressure where it mattered most.

He flipped her to her back, yanking her sweats and panties to her ankles and tossing them across the room. His hot lips kissed her calf.

"Oh no, you don't." She sat up, tugging at his shirt, lifting it over his head. "You have to get naked first."

"You don't have to ask me twice." He believed the key to making the shift in their relationship work was to keep things the same. Saying the words, while huge, didn't have to make things different, even though it was a game changer. He set his pants on the floor near the sleeping bag.

She kissed his chest, curling her fingers around his length.

"Whoa." He hadn't been prepared for her boldness. Of course, he shouldn't have been shocked by it either. She'd always been an incredible and unselfish lover. "What do you think you're doing?"

She glanced up and smiled. "These walls are paper thin. You'll have to be quiet so everyone out there doesn't hear you."

He laughed. "I don't think it's me we'll have to worry about being loud. You're the one who screams when you come."

"I do not." Gently, she pushed him to his back. She stared at him while she tenderly stroked. She'd always been an incredible lover. She'd never been shy in the bedroom and sexually, they'd always been more than compatible. However, since the crash, things for him had been different. He'd held his love so tight to his chest he couldn't fully give himself.

Not to mention the first year his brain injury had changed the way he functioned as a human and a man.

But that had all corrected itself and she'd been a patient and understanding woman.

It amazed him that two people could fight their feelings so hard and yet find themselves so entangled they couldn't let go.

She brought her lips to him, taking the tip into her hot, glorious mouth.

He gritted his teeth, sucking in a deep breath. Pooling her hair on top of her head, he watched as she devoured him in the most torturous pleasure. His toes curled and he wondered how long he could hold out before he lost all control, which he never had much when it came to Kirby.

"I want you—need you—now." She kissed her way up his stomach, straddling his hips.

"Kirby." He swallowed as she guided him deep insider her. Gripping her thighs, he blinked. The room spun while she rolled her body over his in a glorious motion. He reached for her nipples, tugging and twisting.

"Yes." She tossed her head back, moaning. "Please, Wyatt."

He licked his fingers and brought them to her hard nub, rubbing gently while he thrust his hips upward. He could feel her desperation and need. He understood it and wanted to please her in the way she desired. She was all that mattered. All he saw. All he cared about. There was nothing in the world as important as Kirby. Giving her everything she could ever want. Her happiness had become one of the most important things in his life.

Raising up, he sucked her nipple into his mouth, swirling it and grazing it with his teeth. He jerked his hips harder and faster.

"Oh, God. Yes, Wyatt." She wrapped her arms around his shoulders, digging her fingers into his back. Her body convulsed and quivered. Her lips found his in a passionate kiss.

His climax exploded from his body, slamming into hers with the force of a hurricane. A wave of dizziness overcame him. He held her close as he lay back, trying desperately to fill his lungs with oxygen.

He ran his hands up and down her back. The heat of their lovemaking filled the tiny cabin. "So much for you being quiet."

"I wasn't that loud." She rolled to the side, pulling the covers over their bodies. "Besides, I'm sure everyone is sound asleep or listening to the music the Congo makes at night."

"Or you."

She playfully slapped his chest. "Shut up."

"Shit," he mumbled. He couldn't believe he'd been so reckless. "We forgot something."

"Excuse me?"

"Birth control. We didn't use any."

"Fuck." She buried her head in his shoulder. "Not only is that not good, but it's not like us. We've always been so careful."

"It won't happen again, although I didn't pack any."

"I didn't either." She sighed. "I guess you'll be having fun with your hand until we return to the States."

"Trust me, that's no fun at all when you're within a fifty-mile radius." He laughed. He closed his eyes and tried to put the problem out of his mind. There wasn't anything they could do about it. "Go to sleep."

"Wyatt?"

"Hmm?"

"I do you love."

"Why do I feel a but coming?" he asked.

"It's not that. It's just I'm not going to give up a career for anyone. I need to work. It's part of who I am."

He jerked his head. "I would never ask you to."

"I've looked into other grants. Other job positions. Some are in the US. Some are not." She pressed her hand over his mouth. "I haven't applied to any of them. Or given any serious consideration. I was serious when I said I planned to take some time off, but I'm not the kind of person to sit around and do nothing. Studying animals is more than a job. It's a calling."

"I know that better than anyone." He kissed her nose. "Close your eyes and get some sleep."

She might love him, and he didn't doubt that she did, but she wasn't ready to commit and she might never be, something Wyatt would need to wrap his brain around.

And protect his heart.

CHAPTER 9

KIRBY RAISED her finger to her lips. "Relax. Break off a leaf and pretend to eat it." She sat cross-legged on the ground and tried to keep from laughing.

Wyatt had looked terrified on the prop plane. But now that a four-hundred-pound gorilla had plopped down next to him and sniffed his shoulder, he looked as though he might crap his pants. "Not sure how that's going to save me from being mauled to death," he whispered, bringing a leaf to his lips.

Izzy was one of the more trusting and friendly gorillas. She enjoyed human contact. So did her young babies, who rolled around playfully at Wyatt's feet.

Tav, the group's silverback, took his position higher up on the ridge, watching Wyatt. A sadness filled Tav's gaze. Gorillas were fiercely loyal and protective of their own. Like humans, their communities were tightly woven, and they would fight to the death to protect them. Tav wore two new battle scars to prove his bravery.

Pain and sorrow filled Kirby's soul. She'd failed to keep Tav's family safe. Deep down she knew she couldn't have prevented the massacre. If she'd been on-site, she most likely would have been dead, or fighting for her life like Ben.

Her poor assistant.

Tav suddenly jumped to his hind legs on high alert.

"Stay low," Kirby commanded.

All the gorillas scurried, taking off up the ridge. Tav made a defensive move before running down the hill, stopping two feet from where she and Wyatt were sitting. He grunted, pounding his chest, shaking his head.

"What's he doing?" Wyatt whispered.

"I'm not sure," Kirby admitted. "Don't move."

Tav pounded his fist into the ground, then raised it as if to signal toward the west. He narrowed his eyes and lowered his head, grunting.

"What's wrong, my old friend?" she asked as if Tav could answer. She'd developed a relationship with the silverback that had been unprecedented. There was a level of trust that no other human had ever developed with such a male, with one or two exceptions. Tav had allowed her to get incredibly close to him and his family. He treated her as one of his own.

The silverback jerked his head, raised up, pounded his chest, and made what she called the charging noise, which no man ever wanted to hear. She'd been charged before and it was about the scariest thing she'd ever faced in her entire life.

Tav turned and ran up the ridge.

"What the fuck?" Wyatt inched closer. "Was he trying to tell you something?"

"I honestly don't know." She twisted her braid over her shoulder and let out a long breath. "I've never seen him behave in quite that manner. His actions indicated he would charge, but we posed no threat and he knew that, so it makes no sense."

Wyatt reached into his backpack and pulled out his weapon, resting it on his lap. "I know shit about animals, but Hunter works with dogs, and they are good at warning people. Could Tav know something we don't?"

She glanced over her shoulder and shivered. They were thirty minutes from the campgrounds. She'd located Tav and his group five miles from where she'd last seen them before leaving for the States. This didn't surprise her considering the situation. Part of her had worried she might not find them at all. "Do you think someone is out here with us?"

"This is why I didn't want to do this alone." Wyatt stuffed his communication device in his ear and tapped it. "Booker, can you hear me?"

She held her breath, wishing she could listen to

the other side of that conversation. The leaves danced in the slight breeze rolling down the mountainside. Scanning the ridge, she examined the brush for movement.

Nothing.

The gorillas had moved north and west. The campground was south and west. She didn't know if that was good or bad.

The ambassador and his entourage had left for the village about the same time she and Wyatt had begun their hike to find Tav. She'd been given three hours before being told she had to leave. The ambassador had mentioned it was for her own safety. That until they knew exactly what had happened and why, it was best for her to go back to the States.

She got the distinct impression that everyone just wanted her gone and their concern for her well-being wasn't the real reason.

That just pissed her off.

"Something spooked the gorillas. We might have unfriendlies out here," Wyatt said. "Heading back to basecamp. I need a sweep. We're northeast, maybe three miles." He stood, motioning her to follow. "He stayed? That's interesting."

"Who?" she whispered.

"Okay. Keep comms open. See you shortly." Wyatt shifted his gaze left and right as he crossed the ridge. "Ridley didn't leave with the ambassador."

"Why not?"

"Booker's best guess is he got word about something," Wyatt said. "But we both find it strange that he stayed by himself."

"You and your team are here along with six Navy SEALs. That's not alone."

Wyatt chuckled. "That is true. But it makes me wonder if he wasn't ordered to keep a watchful eye over us."

The sound of a twig snapping startled her and she spun on her heel, which caused her to tumble backward, bumping into Wyatt. "Did you hear that?"

"Yeah." He grabbed her waist. "Look up there." He pointed. "Your silverback is following us."

She twisted her body, getting her footing. "The noise came from behind me, not above."

"Could the rest of his clan be following too?" Wyatt tugged her in front of him, spinning in a full three-sixty. He tapped his ear. "Where you at, Booker? Be careful, Kirby's gorillas are keeping in line with us to the north."

"It's possible, but if he felt threatened, he'd run away or go on the offensive. He doesn't normally follow me like this."

"So, you're saying this isn't normal behavior."

"Not necessarily," she said. "Tav could be curious about you. I believe he views me now as one of his own. Since you're with me and not threatening me, he's not attacking, but that doesn't mean he's not feeling protective."

"How will he respond to my team if he runs into them?"

"As long as they stay low, keep their weapons out of sight, and they don't make eye contact with him, they should be fine."

"Fucking wonderful," Wyatt muttered. "I've dealt with snakes, monkeys, and other wildlife in my day, but this is new territory." He adjusted his earpiece and reminded Booker of how he and the rest of the team needed to behave if they came in close proximity of Tav or any other gorilla.

"Tav had to have seen who killed my team," she said.

"Too bad he can't give us that information. It would be helpful right about now." Wyatt stepped in front of her, keeping his gun to his side. "I don't know what makes me more nervous. The fact that I can't see your gorilla anymore or the idea that someone else is out here with us. Do locals come through this area?"

"Other trackers have been known to stroll through."

"What's their primary objective?"

"The good ones are here to help count and keep track of the mountain gorilla population. I know a few of them. One in particular. His name is Zuri. He will report to me or the villages below where the gorilla population is located to help keep the gorillas and humans safe. The bad ones come out here to help the poachers. They do surveillance and sell their services to the poachers."

"How do you tell the difference?" Wyatt asked.

"I've learned over the years not to trust any of them until I get to know them. Trackers who work for the poachers will find where gorillas live and set up traps. They will bring the poachers back to kill the larger animals and catch the babies to sell to private citizens or zoos."

"That's terrible."

"It's a battle I've been fighting for five years. It's never-ending and I know I can't completely stop it, but the work I've done has helped saved so many gorillas from being slaughtered."

Wyatt paused, holding his hand to his ear. "What's that?"

She gripped his biceps.

"Roger that." He glanced over his shoulder. "Booker and Xavier found tracks below us and one mile ahead."

"What kind of tracks?"

"Human," Wyatt said. "Three people. They are following them."

"What should we do?"

"We're going to keep heading toward basecamp. Gunn and Hunter are on this path and two SEALs are above us."

"That leaves Ridley and the local police at camp. I'm not sure I like that. While I've always trusted most locals, I'm not sure I trust them. They have beady eyes," she said.

Wyatt chuckled. "Not sure their steely gaze is why they give me pause, but Ridley is there with them and while I'm still not sure I completely trust the man, we can't find a reason not to."

"Because of Callie?"

"Yup," Wyatt said. "Booker spoke to her on the satphone and while she doesn't know him personally, she did some digging. He appears to be clean."

"Are you ready to tell me what the two of you were chatting about?"

"Nope. Not here." He pushed some brush out of the way. "Come on. We need to get back as fast as possible. We're definitely not alone and we don't want to get caught in any crossfire."

"I don't like being kept in the dark." She followed him, ducking under a few branches. She resented the emerging feeling of betrayal. Wyatt kept telling her that he'd fill her in when the time was right, but that didn't make her growing unease go away. "My entire team is dead and you know more than you're telling me. I have the right to know everything."

"We're not doing this now," he said with a stern tone. "This isn't the time or place."

"Wyatt." She dug her heels into the ground.

He took her by the forearm. "It's not safe. I'm not going to stand here and argue with you. I told you that when it comes to the gorillas, I'd listen to you and do things your way. You need to do the same when it comes to this operation."

"I'm not a child."

"Jesus, Kirby." He nudged her forward. "I'm not saying that you are. You have to let me do my job and right now that entails getting us the fuck out of this spot. Now move."

"Fine." She'd let it go for the moment, but the second they got back to camp, he was going to have to answer her questions.

⁓

Wyatt tossed his rucksack in the back of the chopper. He glanced over his shoulder, half expecting Tav to come racing down the path.

Or maybe whoever had been following them.

Or worse, both the big animal and the bad guys.

Wyatt ran his fingers through his hair and stared at the mountain. His brain worked through a million and one questions with very few answers.

Booker stood, putting the satphone into the case, then strolled in Wyatt's direction. "You doing okay?"

"I've seen better days," Wyatt admitted. A dull headache had haunted him for the last hour. He had no other symptoms, which was a good sign. However, that could change in a heartbeat and that was never good. "I can't believe no one got a read on who the hell was up there with us."

"It's like they vanished." Booker slapped him on the back. "What the hell crawled up Kirby's ass? She's been in a pissy mood for the last hour."

Wyatt let out a long breath as he peered into the helicopter. Kirby had already climbed in and taken a seat in the back near Ridley, most likely pumping the poor man for information that he wasn't about to give up. "She's angry at me."

Booker arched a brow. "The two of you looked pretty damn cozy this morning. What the fuck happened?"

"She knows I'm keeping something from her and now she's making me pay for it."

"About what we suspect Ben was up to?" Booker asked.

Wyatt nodded. "Among other things."

"You could probably read her in on some of it."

"I didn't want to do it here, with so many ears listening and not knowing who understands English." Wyatt kept his voice low. "We know nothing about the locals. But also because she's too close to the situation. She trusted Ben and he betrayed her. She's not going to take that piece of information easily. Not to mention we don't know if it's true or to what extent. For all we know, he was forced somehow. I'm also concerned that Ridley didn't leave with the ambassador and stayed with us. It doesn't sit well, and I will keep all this information to myself until I know exactly why he did that."

"I just got off the horn with Callie and she learned another DEA agent is meeting the ambassador in the village."

"It would have been nice if he told us that."

"That's just it. The agent is undercover. Callie pulled some major strings to find that out. She's not sure Ridley even knows because they are different cases, but since this shit went down, the DEA thought they'd cross streams. Ridley's job is placating the ambassador, making sure we leave. We're not welcome here, but the ambassador can't come out and say that. He's got to pretend to fight to have us here." Booker tapped his fist against the bird. "Callie learned from a friend of hers that this situation is becoming hostile between the two governments. That our presence is making the locals nervous. They don't believe we're here to help solve the problem but create a different one. It's now completely out of our hands."

"Have you spoken to Stone?"

Booker nodded. "He says we can stay in-country for now, but to be prepared to be pulled at any given moment. The politicians are doing their thing to protect their interests and the Department of Defense needs to make sure there isn't any fallout."

"That means this could go down as gorilla poaching, even if it's not." Wyatt had been on enough unsanctioned missions to know the drill. "I can't let that happen. I know Kirby. She won't rest until she has answers and someone is behind bars."

"Her passion is commendable and her heart is in the right place, but sometimes that will get you killed."

"You're not helping," Wyatt muttered. "Any news on Ben?"

"Still critical," Booker said. "The plan is to move him to Germany but there needs to be improvement in his condition. However, the government here doesn't want to move him until they've had a chance to question him regarding what happened. The ambassador is inclined to agree."

"Why the fuck would he do that? Ben is a United States citizen. You'd think they'd want him Stateside. Hell, I'm sure Ridley and his team want that. That would give them more power."

"But Ridley and the DEA might have different goals than the ambassador," Booker said. "If the ambassador has anything to do with helping to smuggle guns and drugs in and out of this country and is aiding in poaching, he'll want Ben to pay the price here. He'll want this to end here and be done with it. Take it back to the States where Ben can sing like a fucking canary, it's all over."

"That's not the ambassador's job."

"Come on, Wyatt. You know how these things work. Or do I need to remind you about the time my team flew in to save your SEAL team's ass? You were caught between a rock and a hard place when you thought you were on a search and rescue mission, but the man you were looking for turned traitor."

"I don't ever want to be reminded of that shit show." Wyatt rubbed the back of his neck.

The rest of their team jogged across the clearing, tossing their bags in the back of the other bird.

"How long will it take the ambassador and everyone with him to get to the village?"

"According to Kirby, she said about four hours by Jeep."

Wyatt glanced at his watch. "If we leave now, we can get there about the same time."

"What are we waiting for?" Booker smiled. "Are you going to be my copilot, or do you want to ride in the back?"

"I think I'm safer up front with you. Kirby might bite my head off if she doesn't inundate me with questions."

Booker laughed. "Trust me, man. Avoidance isn't going to make her go any easier on you when you tell her the truth. Might as well swallow the horse pill like a big boy in a grown-up relationship."

"You're a pain in my ass, you know that?" Wyatt hoisted himself into the chopper and strapped himself in. He turned and gave Kirby a smile.

She more or less smirked.

That kind of said it all.

Booker fired up the chopper. It rattled like an old

tin can, but that didn't bother Wyatt. Not this time. Booker was in the cockpit. Even if they went down, it would be in a blaze of glory.

Out of the corner of his eye, he noticed a shiny reflection in the trees. "Oh, fuck. Get this bird up in the air now." He strapped on his head gear. "Check. Check. Xavier, you read."

Four loud pops filled the air.

"Loud and clear," Xavier said.

"Both SEALs are down." Fuck. "Cover me." There was no way Wyatt would leave any military man, but especially not a SEAL behind.

"I'll hover, but hurry the fuck up, man," Booker said.

"I got your back." Gunn sat in the opening, weapon at the ready.

"Me too," Hunter said through the comms.

Xavier lifted from the ground and once he cleared the treetops, he banked right.

As soon as Wyatt's feet hit the ground, Booker eased the helicopter in the air. Gunn and Hunter fired more shots into the tree line.

The sound of machine guns filled his ears. "Motherfuckers." He raced across the clearing. Both SEALs crawled in his direction.

"Got me in the leg twice. I can get to the chopper," one said.

The other one was a few paces behind and didn't look as good.

Wyatt glanced toward Xavier and signaled. The SEAL had two wounds in the center of his gut. That was never good. Wyatt ripped off his shirt and placed pressure on the wound. "Can you hold this?"

"I can try, sir," the sailor said.

"This is going to hurt." Wyatt tucked his arms under the SEAL's pits. That's when he noticed the trail of blood. Fuck. The bullets had torn right through the man's body.

"We need to fly up to basecamp," Booker's voice came over the comms. "There are four SEALs up there unprotected. We can't leave them."

"Get Wyatt," Xavier said. "These men are retreating. I'll do a sweep up the ridge."

"Fire a line of shots between us before you get too far. I'll follow shortly," Booker said.

Wyatt had listened to the exchange and waved to Booker. "You're going to be okay," he said to one of the sailors as he examined the wound. The man with the belly wound had lost a shit ton of blood. He was pale and his pulse was weak. They would need to head down the mountain as soon as possible.

He shifted his attention to the other SEAL. His wounds weren't as bad, but his leg didn't look good.

"Bring the bird down," Wyatt commanded. "I need a medic kit."

"I can help," Ridley appeared at the side of the chopper along with Kirby.

Gently, Wyatt lifted SEAL one into the helicopter.

"Check the first aid kit for a saline drip." He hoisted SEAL two over his shoulder and heaved himself inside. "Go, go, go."

"I'm going to trim more trees and fly up the ridgeline," Booker said in that way-too-fucking-calm voice of his. Actually, it wasn't calm. It was as if he were in the throes of passion, because that man got off on flying like a fucking maniac. It wasn't like he had a death wish, far from it. Booker enjoyed life and wanted to keep on living. He also wanted to make sure all his passengers survived to tell the story. But he got some weird thrill by banking left, then right, then nose down. And the damn fucking trees. He loved that shit more than anything.

"Anyone else but me notice that the two locals are long gone?" Wyatt rummaged through the first aid kit. He made a tourniquet out of his belt and strapped it around the SEAL's leg.

He screamed. "Fuck me."

"Sorry, man. We've got to stop the bleeding," Wyatt said.

"What about my buddy?" the SEAL asked.

The sound of gunfire in the distance rang out.

Ridley hung out the side of the chopper, firing off his own rounds.

"I'm going to go check on your friend." Wyatt patted the sailor's leg. "Kirby, I need you to give me a hand."

"With what?" Kirby scooted across the floor of the chopper as it flew low across the mountain.

"There are two clear exit wounds." Wyatt pressed his head to the SEAL's chest. "Sir, can you take a couple of deep breaths for me?"

"Hurts like hell, but sure." The SEAL did as he was asked.

"It sounds as though you have a gurgle. I don't know if that's from a cracked rib or if one of the bullets went through your lung," Wyatt said. "But you're going to bleed out if I don't do something. So, we're going to stitch you up."

"We?" Kirby stared at him with wide eyes.

"Yup. Right after I start this drip."

"How do you know how to do all this?" Kirby asked.

"Because we've all almost died a time or two," Booker yelled over the roar of the engines.

Machine gun fire erupted.

"We're pushing them down the mountain," Xavier said over the comms. "I've got the four SEALs in view. You've got to get them so I can keep these assholes from making it to basecamp."

"Ridley, can you handle the ladder to pull up four passengers?" Booker asked.

"You got it." Ridley set his weapon aside and found the rope ladder.

"This is even better." Wyatt held up a tube of glue.

"You're going to superglue him together?" Kirby asked.

The sailor laughed, then coughed. "Fuck that hurts." He cleared his throat. "Sorry, ma'am."

"Don't apologize. She's got the mouth of five truck drivers." Wyatt smiled, handing her the glue. "You do this and I'll do the drip. Start with his back. Clean up the blood and wound as best you can first."

The helicopter shifted as the first man jumped onto the ladder.

"We've got a breach. It will be six minutes before they are at the campgrounds," Xavier said. "Hurry the fuck up."

"As soon as the last SEAL is on the ladder, I can start up the ridge; that should buy a few minutes," Booker said.

"Okay, his back is done," Kirby said.

"Good. Now the belly." Wyatt tied off the sailor's upper arm while he found a vein for the fluids. Quickly, he slid the needle in the man's arm and released the tourniquet. "That should keep you stable." He inched toward the front of the bird and found the satphone. It was time to call this in.

"We're going to start climbing. Signal to the men below to get their asses on board," Booker said.

"I've got it." Ridley nodded.

Wyatt pressed the satphone to his ear. "Stone? Can you hear me?"

"What the fuck is going on over there?"

"We were ambushed. Two of the SEAL team are wounded," Wyatt said. "They need transport to a hospital. I'm no doctor, but they might make it to Germany."

"Tell Stone we've only got enough gas in this bird to get us back to the main town about thirty miles from the village," Booker said.

"Did you hear that?" Wyatt shifted, making room for the rest of the SEAL team as they climbed on board.

"Yeah. I got it. I'll contact the Navy," Stone said.

"Any chance you can keep this out of the press and away from the ambassador?" Wyatt asked.

Silence on the other end.

Wyatt pinched the bridge of his nose. "Stone?"

"I'm processing that request."

"I wouldn't ask if I didn't think it was imperative," Wyatt said.

"It won't stay hidden long. It will get out, or at the very least the ambassador will learn of what happened." Stone's words hit Wyatt right in the center of his heart.

"It's a risk we need to take," Wyatt said.

"All right. I'll see what I can do. In the meantime, head toward our third checkpoint. That's a safer bet than the main town and a little closer."

"Roger that." Wyatt rubbed his temples.

"Hold on," Booker said. "Let's get these men to a safe place."

Wyatt glanced to the front of the chopper as it banked hard to the left and down the mountainside, taking off three treetops.

He'd never been so happy to be in the air in all his life.

CHAPTER 10

Wyatt stood outside the hotel and scanned the streets with Hunter at his side. Kirby was still upstairs changing after taking the longest shower in history.

"I get the feeling that ambush wasn't just about us," Hunter said. "Whoever that was wanted the SEAL team gone too."

"Agreed." Wyatt's mind filled with more questions he couldn't answer and that gave him a headache. All the doctors warned him about overstimulation of his brain and how that could affect his ability to concentrate. But the part that worried him the most was the throbbing that had developed between his temples. It wasn't a sharp pain, which would indicate an ice-pick migraine. That would be a precursor to a full-on migraine that he couldn't afford. But the dull sensation still caused him to pause and slow down his thoughts. He needed to make sure he fired on all cylinders or he wasn't doing his team any favors. "However, what's the point in doing that? We didn't find any evidence that indicated anything other than poaching."

"I got the impression the ambassador wanted to push that agenda," Hunter said. "I overheard him talking to one of his people that he wasn't surprised by the brutality of the attack. That Kirby and her team made a lot of enemies. He mentioned warning her that her outspoken attitude was going to get her in trouble."

"The mountain gorillas are a protected species. Poaching is illegal. She and her team should have been protected." Wyatt shifted his gaze up and down the street. "This Kofi guy has to be associated with Okra."

"If Okra wants payback for crippling his operation and is using Kofi and his men to achieve that goal, then why didn't they take you and Kirby out when they had the chance?"

"That's if they were the ones watching us," Wyatt said. "It was as if the gorillas shuffled us back to basecamp. Like they knew something was coming and guided us to safety."

"Who else could have been out there?"

"Kirby told me about a local tracker named Zuri who helps her sometimes, but for the life of me I can't figure out why he wouldn't have made himself known if he was there."

"There were three sets of human tracks that circled where you and Kirby had been sitting with the gorillas. We didn't get to follow them too far because we needed to leave, but they came from high up on the ridge."

"I counted eight men with guns that came down the mountain," Wyatt said. "But that included the locals."

Hunter arched a brow.

"Yeah. They were well hidden, but I caught sight of one of them when I pulled the injured SEALs onto the chopper."

"Fuck. So they were sitting there waiting. But again, why wait? They could have attacked before we loaded our birds."

"A crash is easier to cover up. Having to explain more American deaths would be a political nightmare. But if two helicopters go down due to malfunction or pilot error, that can be explained away as a tragedy."

"That's fucked up." Hunter glanced over his shoulder. "Here comes Kirby."

"Don't say anything to her about this conversation. Not yet anyway. I need to let it all percolate in my head."

"She's asking a lot of questions and honestly, she deserves the truth."

Wyatt nodded. He didn't want to keep anything from Kirby, but he didn't want her going off half-cocked either. "I'm not sure her staying in-country is the right move."

"If it's her they want, then the only way to catch the assholes is to use what we have."

This was the last thing Wyatt wanted to hear, even if he knew it was the truth. "All the more reason to keep her in the dark about a few things for now."

"I respectfully disagree, man. Knowledge is power." Hunter squeezed his shoulder. "I will follow your lead. I know you care about her and want to protect her, but you're making a mistake by not telling her everything."

"I'll take it under advisement."

Kirby strolled through the main doors. Booker was two steps behind.

"I need to pick up a few things at the market," Kirby said.

"All right. Let's go." Wyatt curled his fingers through hers.

She glared. "I'm capable of going myself."

"You're not going anywhere alone," he said. "Safety in numbers."

"I could use a stroll through town." Booker smiled. "I'm hungry anyway."

"Fine." Kirby yanked her hand free. "You two lovebirds can tag along if you must." She took off down the street.

Wyatt sighed. He might be in the doghouse for long time.

~

KIRBY STROLLED through the market and did her best to ignore Wyatt and his sidekick. Her frustration was at an all-time high. Fear prickled her senses. Whenever poachers came after her gorillas in the past, they had never attacked her personally. Her team members had been injured trying to protect the gorillas, but no one had been murdered.

She'd been warned and even threatened, but nothing had ever come of those. The worst attack had been right before she'd installed the security cameras which Ben had warned her not to do. He believed it would cause her more trouble than they were worth. She never understood his reasoning. Catching the leaders of the ring could only be seen as a good thing in her eyes where Ben believed it to be an antagonistic move. He thought a better approach was to let the authorities handle everything.

Maybe he wouldn't be in the hospital fighting for his life if she'd listened.

Wyatt and Booker questioned his loyalty. Wyatt especially wondered about the medical supply run, but Ben wasn't upset about her changing plans. He shrugged his shoulders and acted as if it were no big deal. He could come to the States another time.

The fact that Wyatt refused to tell her what he'd learned from Ridley or what he was thinking regarding the latest events made her want to wring his handsome neck. He had no right to keep her in the dark.

She curled her fingers around Wyatt's biceps. "There's Sally. I want to go say hello."

"Okay, but don't wander where I can't see you," Wyatt said. "Booker and I will be right here enjoying whatever this is we're eating and drinking." He pulled out a chair in front of the café where they'd just purchased some local cuisine. "I'm not kidding, Kirby. We don't know if we've been followed and you're a bit of a local celebrity. I'm sure word is out that you're in town."

"I'm just going to be right over there," she said. "Back in a few." She scurried off, dashing between a few people. "Sally, it's me, Kirby."

"Oh, hey, Kirby." Sally smiled.

"I'm glad to see you again." Kirby stood by the street vendor with her bag of goodies to bring back to the hotel. "How are things going with the story?"

"It's not great, to be honest." Sally tucked her short hair behind her ears. "The ambassador is pushing hard for me to be done with it."

"What do you mean? There's been no arrest. No chatter as to what group even did this."

Sally glanced over her shoulder before taking Kirby by the arm. "I was hoping I'd have the chance to run into you. I was going to try to track you down, but I have to be discreet."

"What's going on?"

"I don't believe this is *just* about poaching. I mean, it is. The market for gorillas is huge. But you don't need me to tell you that." Sally's gaze shifted left and right. "The ambassador wants me to report the story as an unfortunate tragedy and how the government here is doing everything they can to protect the mountain gorilla and those who study them. He wants me to leave. He sees no reason to follow up until the culprits are caught."

"That makes no sense," Kirby said. "What about my team? What about getting justice for them?"

"That's what I said. American citizens were murdered. In cold blood. But the thing is, we don't have any images of that."

"Excuse me?" She blinked. Her heart dropped to her toes. "I thought the SEALs took photographs. I thought that was all documented. It was an ambush. My team didn't even see them coming. That's what I was told."

"Same. I was told I would be given access to the official report, but when it came to my email this morning, the ambassador apologized for only having the written report, stating that the government couldn't release the images."

"Wyatt needs to hear this." Kirby turned her head, waving frantically to Wyatt.

He jumped from his seat and raced through the maze of people. "What's wrong?"

"Sally was just telling me that there are no photographs of my team after the ambush."

"I was only given a report regarding the attack, which is the ambassador's report. That's what he wants me to go on air with," Sally said.

"And what exactly does he want you to say?"

"Basically, that Kirby's team died because they got in the way of poachers. That the local government is doing everything they can to end poaching," Sally said. "He's downplaying the murder of the team. But that's not even my biggest issue. When I spoke with my husband, his contacts with the Department of Defense informed him there's more to this story, though they couldn't elaborate. And I know Ridley isn't here for shits and giggles." Sally raised her hand. "I came here to chase a story about drugs and guns being trafficked in and out of this country. Ridley is DEA. It doesn't take a genius to connect the dots."

"If that's the case, how did you land on a poaching story?" Wyatt asked.

"I was told by a tracker that someone at Kirby's camp was the contact." Sally held Kirby's gaze.

"That's impossible." Kirby clenched her fists. "No one on my team would do that. Besides, how would they get them in? There are only two people who make supply runs. You are staring at one. The other is fighting for his life."

Wyatt rested a strong hand on her shoulder.

She shrugged it off. "Don't you fucking touch me." She sucked in a deep breath.

"It makes sense, Kirby," Wyatt said. He'd been running on this theory all along.

"This was what you and Ridley were talking about, wasn't it?" she asked.

"I can't get into that with you," Wyatt said with a tight lip.

"Because you don't want to? Because you don't think I can handle it?" She crossed her arms over her chest.

"I'm sure it has more to do with the fact I'm standing here," Sally offered. "I'm the media and sometimes seen as the enemy, but I can assure you, I'm not. The ambassador is hiding something. Maybe covering his own ass. Based on what I've seen, I'm guessing he could even be part of the operation. At the very least, he allows it to happen for his own personal gain." Sally adjusted her bag over her shoulder. "I heard an incident occurred and two SEALs were injured, but I can't get any intel on that. I'm being told that it was an unfortunate accident between them and the locals."

"Not at all what happened," Wyatt said. "But our government isn't going to start a conflict, not if it can be avoided. They will publicly spin it how they have to, while they internally deal it with differently."

"So what the fuck are they doing about it?" Kirby

planted her hands on her hips and glared. "And you better start telling me everything or you'll sleep with Booker tonight."

"That's a question for Ridley and trust me, I will ask," Wyatt said.

"Why don't you let me interview you about what happened today on the mountain?" Sally asked.

"I can't." Wyatt threaded his fingers through his hair.

"Why not?" Sally tilted her head.

"The organization I work for won't allow it."

"What about me? I was there. I saw everything. I watched Wyatt save two Navy SEALs," Kirby said. "There's nothing preventing me from telling the truth of what really happened up there."

"That's going to piss off two governments, not to mention a drug and gun trafficker that wants you dead." Wyatt shook his head. "It's not smart. Not unless I can get Ridley and the Brotherhood Protectors to sign off on it."

"I'm willing to play by certain rules," Sally said. "I don't want to do anything that would jeopardize the investigation or put anyone else in danger. However, the public does have the right to know what's really happening here." She dug into her bag, pulling out a card. "You can reach me at that number. I'll be here for at least two nights."

"I don't need your permission to give an interview." Kirby had spent her entire adult life doing exactly what she wanted, instead of what her parents thought she should be doing. Her father wanted her to find a nice suitable husband and settle down into being a wife and mother.

Her mom wanted the same thing.

They both believed a woman's role was to serve her man. That her career would eventually fall to the wayside because she'd have children and they would become the center of her life.

The kind of life her parents had wasn't for her. They weren't happy people. If they were, her father wouldn't be having one affair after the other and her mother wouldn't be spending her days pretending her husband wasn't such a shit. Deep down, she knew her parents were fundamentally decent people. They were trapped by their ideals. By what they believed their lives should be instead of what their lives could be.

She would never allow her world to be like that again. She'd fallen into that once when she'd been in college. Never again.

Her relationship with Wyatt had given her the freedom to be herself. To chase her dreams.

Now that they were a couple in every sense of the word, it didn't give him the right to dictate what she did or how she did it. If that's how it was going to be, it ended right here.

"That's right, you don't. But I'm asking you to

wait until I have three conversations." Wyatt lowered his chin.

"Three? Who else do you need to call besides your boss and Ridley?"

"A contact I have in the military. If there's more to this, they will know. I've tried reaching him once but haven't gotten through. Let me try again before you do anything," Wyatt said.

"And are you going to fill me in on everything?" Kirby asked.

"Not standing out here, I'm not." Wyatt gripped her forearm. "We'll be in touch, Sally. It was good to see you again." He guided her back in the direction of Booker.

"I want to know now and you better not leave anything out."

"Up in the room, and you've made that sentiment perfectly clear," Wyatt said with an exasperated sigh.

CHAPTER 11

Kirby plopped herself back on the bed and stared at the poor excuse for a fan. "I find it hard to believe Ben was running drugs and guns right under my nose."

"Don't take this wrong, but you're singularly focused." Wyatt kicked off his shoes and leaned against the door. "I looked into Ben's background."

She bolted upright. "So did I. He's worked with mountain gorillas before. He was in a different part of the Congo with a different animal behavior specialist."

"I'm aware."

"So, you know he was dedicated to the cause."

"Or dedicated to *his cause*." Wyatt arched a brow. "He left that post six months before applying to work with you. His reason for leaving was because he was so impressed with you. But when I read Doctor Antel's discharge of him, it wasn't glowing."

"They had fundamental differences," Kirby said. "Antel has a different philosophy. He doesn't approach the gorillas the same way I do. I use techniques much like Dian Fossey, where Antel prefers to study at a much further distance. It's not wrong, but Ben wanted to be closer."

"Or maybe he just wanted you to be closer so he could continue smuggling."

"I don't know, maybe," she said.

"Didn't you tell me he constantly asked to let him take the supply runs off your hands? And that he went to the States two times a year for other reasons. However, each time he went, it still became official business for you."

"The only way you'd know that is if you went through my business." She lowered her chin and arched a brow. "You're full of secrets, aren't you?"

"You know everything that I do."

"But you lied to me."

"No. I didn't. I told you that I would tell you when the time was right." Wyatt pushed from the door and sat on the edge of the mattress. "My team and I are still trying to piece everything together and there are so many holes. Too many unknowns. My job was to come here, find out what happened, and protect you. If that meant I had to keep a few things to myself to do it, then you can't fault me for that."

"But you, of all people, know how I feel about lying."

"Kirby, this isn't the same thing." He took her hand and kissed her palm. "We both have trust issues. I understand that mine are very different and have nothing to do with cheating or being lied to by a partner. Or what your ex-boyfriend put you through when he found out you were pregnant. I'm not that man."

"It doesn't matter." Her eyes burned with tears. "It's still a betrayal. Those people were my responsibility. Put yourself in my shoes. Imagine how you'd feel if I kept the fact that one of your team could have been doing something nefarious behind your back."

"Come on, Kirby. I put that bug in your ear before we even left the States."

"Maybe so, but you learned more when we got here and I should have been the first to know. Especially after…" She let her words trail off. Flashes of college filled her mind. It had taken a lot to tell her ex she'd loved him. That hadn't come easy for her because of her parents. Being in a committed relationship felt like a trap.

Being pregnant had been something unexpected, but for a fleeting moment, family life had been something she thought she wanted. Desired.

And it was taken from her the second she opened her dorm room.

For a hot minute she'd thought about raising that

baby alone, but her ex wouldn't allow it. He wanted to be involved if they weren't going to get married. Hell, he wanted more. He wanted that child to himself. To raise with the woman he really loved.

Her roommate.

That was never going to happen.

So she did what she thought was her only option at the time.

A decision that still brought tears to her eyes.

"After we said we loved each other?" Wyatt asked. "Because this doesn't change that."

"Doesn't it, though? How can I trust you now?" Her heart felt heavy. Part of her knew she was being unreasonable, but fear wouldn't allow her to let it go. This had been the entire reason she'd kept him at arm's length for so long. He was exactly the kind of man she could fall in love with and that's exactly what happened.

"Because you know deep down that I was always going to tell you." He palmed her cheek, forcing her to gaze into his soulful eyes. "I love you, Kirby. I have for a long time. I've been as afraid of this commitment as you have. I don't want to lose you either because some asshole kills you, or over the fact that I chose to keep intel to myself until it was safe to tell you."

"It's not just that. You told everyone *but* me."

He stood, raking a hand angrily across the top of his head. "Those men are putting their lives on the line for you. It's different and you know it. I can't keep apologizing or having this argument with you. I've told you everything. Ridley and my contact are getting us the official statement the government will release and what they agree is okay for you to say. I have it on good authority by Ridley that you will be pleased with it." He curled his fingers around the doorknob. "I'll be bunking with Booker if you need me. Don't open this door for anyone but me or my team. One of us will be on watch in the hallway all night. And don't leave this room without an escort, got it?"

She nodded and watched the only man she'd ever truly loved slip out into the hallway. She lay back on the bed and closed her eyes. She shouldn't have let him leave, but if for no other reason, she needed a good cry, alone.

∽

"Make sure she doesn't leave," Wyatt said.

Gunn narrowed his stare. "You're not staying in there with her?"

"It's a long story, and I don't wish to discuss it." Wyatt tapped on Booker's door. "Open up."

"What the fuck are you doing here?" Booker stood in the middle of the room in his boxers.

"Having a goddamned sleepover because, for the life of me, I don't understand women."

"I could have told you that." Booker stepped to the side. "But there's only one bed in here, and I'm not sleeping on that sofa."

"I'll manage just fine on that ugly thing. Toss me a pillow and a blanket."

"What the fuck did you do?" Booker threw a pillow and a ratty old throw thing that had seen better days. "She can't still be mad at you about the whole Ridley thing."

"She says she can't trust me anymore because of it, which is bullshit. I get why she's pissed. It has to do with shit in her past and her parents." Wyatt fell back on the sofa that barely held his weight. "I can't get into it because that would be breaking a confidence, and I wouldn't do that to her, but I can't reason with her because of it."

"Then don't." Booker eased back into bed, pulling the comforter over his legs. "One thing I've learned being with Callie is that sometimes words are hollow. They're sounds that come from your mouth. You must show her you're not the past or her parents." Booker punched his pillow and leaned against the headboard.

"It's not as simple as that. What I did isn't anything like what she's comparing it to. It's apples to oranges."

"Ever think she's afraid so at the first sign of trouble, she pushes you away and you let her do it? You're letting her believe you're exactly like whoever or whatever she's set up in her mind. If you want her, you'll have to fight for her, and sleeping on that sofa isn't the way to do it." Booker arched a brow. "Telling her you love her is one thing. Showing her that you'll be there for her for the long haul no matter what happens is something entirely different."

Wyatt jumped to his feet. His friend was right. Walking out of the room was as if he'd given up and tossed in the white towel.

Booker chuckled.

"I'm not going back there because I think you're a genius. I don't want to sleep on this godawful couch, listening to you snore."

"Whatever you say, man. Just whatever you do, don't come back."

"I'll see you in the morning." Wyatt stepped out into the hallway. "Not one fucking peep out of you." He pointed to Gunn.

Gunn raised his hands. "Wasn't going to say a word." He laughed. "Enjoy your night. Someone might as well."

"Fuck off," Wyatt muttered. He reached in his pocket for his key. "Shit." He'd left it inside his room. He tapped his knuckles on the door. "Kirby, it's Wyatt. Open the door."

It took a good minute before she did as requested.

"What do you want?" She turned her back to him, wiping her face.

Fuck, the last thing he wanted was for her to be crying.

He closed the door, locked it, and leaned against the wood, stuffing his hands in his pockets. He sucked at relationships. His life had been his career. His family had been his team. Having one special person in his life hadn't been a priority until Kirby strolled in. She had changed everything. It hadn't happened overnight. But for the last seven years, she'd been the air that he breathed. She was the first person he thought of when he opened his eyes and the last person whom his mind drifted off to at night. His dreams were filled with her images.

"I want you," he whispered. "I understand why you're upset. I get it's a trigger. I really do. But what I don't comprehend is why you're pushing me away so hard and I'm not going to let you do it. Not unless you tell me you don't love me and you don't want to be with me."

Slowly, she faced him. Her eyes were puffy and that broke his heart.

He pushed from the door and inched closer.

"I need not only to be treated as an equal, but I need to feel it and it's the latter that's missing."

"I never intended to do that to you."

"Those men might be your team." She pointed toward the door. "But I'm here with you, risking my life just as much. I deserve to be in the know as much as they do and yet you treated me with kid gloves just because of a sense of duty or because you didn't think I could handle it. My entire childhood was built on other people making decisions for me. My ex wanted to control my career. Our lives. It's that kind of powerlessness that I can't tolerate."

"Okay. I get it. I will do better. I won't keep things out of trying to protect you or your feelings again."

Her eyes went wide. "Just like that. You're all of a sudden going to tell me everything when it happens."

"Will you meet me halfway to know that I promise to tell you when I can? That the only reason I don't tell you something is because someone else is tying my hands?"

"I need to know exactly what that means."

"Ridley or the government. They might require me to keep my trap shut."

She tugged at the clip that held her hair in a ponytail. "That's a hard pill to swallow, but I guess I can live with that."

He wrapped his arms around her waist and pulled her close. "I'm sorry."

"It's okay. I forgive you."

"We'll find out who killed your team and nail those bastards to the wall. I promise you that." He kissed her forehead.

She rested her head on his chest. "Sadly, I'm afraid my assistant had something to do with it and I'm the fool who didn't see any of it."

"You're no fool, Kirby Carrington." He stroked

her hair. "You are kind, loving, and passionate. Ben took advantage of your blind spot. It happens to the best of us."

She tilted her head. "It's never happened to you."

"Oh yes, it has." He cupped her face and brushed his mouth over her sweet lips. "Me and my genius brain got taken for a ride by a pretty lady once. She saw two of my weaknesses. The first, hating when anyone takes advantage of another person, and the second, my enjoyment of gadgets. I ended up helping her hack into her ex's computer system. I almost helped her steal from him before I figured out what was going on."

"No way." Kirby smiled. "Who was this chick?"

"Some girl I was dating in the Naval Academy. I thought I was in love with her, but I realized I had been more enamored with saving her when it ended." Wyatt took Kirby's hand and led her to the bed. "I've never had to save you and that's one of the things that attracted me to you in the first place. You're strong and fiercely independent. You don't need me, but sometimes it would be nice if you did."

"Oh, Wyatt. I do need you." She snuggled in next to him, wrapping her arms and legs around his body. "More importantly I want and love you."

"So glad we got that cleared up." He clicked off the light. "I've been thinking about how to catch these bad guys and a plan has been forming, but I don't like what the most logical thing to do is."

"And what's that?"

"Use you as bait."

"It's me they want," she whispered.

"I know, but I don't know this country and they do. They have the upper hand. But if I can drag their asses to Yellowstone, I'll have the upper hand and beat them at their own game."

"How would you do that?" She rested her chin on his chest.

"By making them think we've packed up and gone home. Protection detail over. Let them think they've won and you've moved on."

"I'm still not quite following."

He brushed the hair from her face. "What if we set you up to study the wolves? Make them think you're all alone somewhere and have them come to you where they think they can make it look like you died in some freak wolf mauling or other accident. Poaching happens all the time with wolves. People die accidentally by gunshots. I'm sure with Stone's contacts, he could help you find a local organization that could use someone like you, if only temporary. We could use Sally to create a false narrative, reporting a story about you setting up in Yellowstone and all the dangers there."

"While you catch the bad guys?"

"Something like that," Wyatt said.

"My God. You really are a fucking genius."

"I have my moments." He chuckled. "But now I

have to get everyone else to sign off on it." He closed his eyes. The plan was a good one. It would take time, but done right, it would bring the bad guys right to his doorstep.

Where he had control.

And Kirby at his side.

CHAPTER 12

Kirby had never liked being the center of attention. Giving interviews had been something she avoided. She only did them when they served a greater purpose. In the five years she lived in the Congo, she'd done four. They were solely focused on her work with the mountain gorillas and were for either raising money for her cause or to raise awareness regarding poaching and they weren't for news feeds. They were for magazines and organizations that supported her efforts.

She sat in a chair in the small conference room of the hotel with a mic clipped to her blouse and more makeup than she'd worn in her entire life.

"Relax." Sally leaned over and patted her knee. "Wyatt and his team have taken care of everything."

"I know." She flipped her hair over her shoulder.

She wished she'd put it in a ponytail. "It's hard to believe he could set everything up in a day."

"His organization has connections everywhere, and Ridley is a surprising man. When I first met him, I didn't like him. He cockblocked me at every turn. But that's his job. The media is often at odds with people like him. They believe we get in their way and sometimes we do. Our objectives are a little different. I want to report to the public where he wants to keep things quiet."

"I can see now where sometimes that's a necessary evil."

"I wouldn't normally go along with a game like this, but my husband thinks it's a good idea," Sally said. "However, I was a little surprised my producer went along with it."

"Why?"

"While we're reporting on facts and we're not lying to the public, it's still a bit of a manipulation and abuse of our power." Sally leaned back, letting her makeup people powder her face. "Don't get me wrong, I would have gone rogue and done it anyway. I've been chasing the drug and gun trafficking story for two years. It saddens me to no end that it has been attached to the poaching, and what happened to your team and gorillas sickens me. I'm happy to play a role in bringing these bastards down."

"If this works, I don't know how I'll ever repay you."

The makeup woman scurried away.

Sally sat up taller, fiddling with her blouse and glancing in Wyatt's direction.

"I understand that you won't be coming back. That your grant is over and your work here is done. But you're an amazing woman with such a passion for animals. I'm sure this temporary gig Wyatt set up for you could turn into something spectacular. Not to mention that man is madly in love with you. Living your life will be all the payment I will ever need."

"We're all set," the cameraman said. "Ready whenever you are."

"Let's do this thing." Sally smiled. "Roll the cameras."

Kirby rolled her neck and did her best not to look like she swallowed a bowl of lemons.

"This is Sally Weidmore reporting from the Congo with Kirby Carrington, an animal behaviorist who has been living here for the last five years studying the mountain gorilla. This is my second interview with Kirby in a two-part series. Thanks for taking the time, Kirby. I know you have limited time today as you're heading back to the States."

"Thank you for having me," Kirby said. "I appreciate it."

"My pleasure." Sally glanced at her notepad. "Last time we spoke it was up at your campgrounds when you returned right after finding out your entire team had been killed during a poaching raid."

"It was a tragic loss. I'm devastated. There was no reason for it."

"I understand that the authorities have yet to make any arrests. About five months ago, you had cameras installed that helped the authorities capture poachers the last time this happened. You mentioned this time the cameras were destroyed as well as any images. Could this have been an inside job?"

"I can't speak too publicly on that, but it's possible. It saddens me that the authorities aren't doing more." Kirby tried to rein in her anger and keep to the script. She hoped her facial expressions didn't give away her true feelings. Wyatt had spent two hours reviewing the interview with her before she ever sat down with Sally.

"Will you be making an addendum to the book you recently turned into your publisher, covering the recent events?"

"Absolutely," Kirby said. "It's imperative that the world understands what's really happening here. This wasn't only about poaching."

"What do you mean?"

"I believe there has been a drug and gun smuggling operation running through my foundation," Kirby said. "I wish I had seen it sooner and that I could have prevented the lives that were lost."

"Do you have proof of this?"

"Not yet and unfortunately, I must leave the country. I'm hoping that this interview will help engage the local government to take the allegations more seriously and look closer at the problem so they can shut it down."

"Do you believe that both governments are working together?"

"That's a question for them." Kirby nodded like a bobblehead. "I've spoken to the ambassador, and as you know, he visited my campgrounds. Unfortunately, I'm not sure I'm being heard. The focus is on the poaching, which trust me, is a huge problem, but I believe there is a bigger issue, and I hope someone steps up to the plate and does something."

"We appreciate you shedding some light on this horrible situation," Sally said. "You've been such a big component in helping preserve and grow the mountain gorilla population. I'm sure my viewers wonder what's next for Kirby Carrington."

"I'm so glad you asked me that question." Kirby wiggled in her chair, excitement bubbling in her chest. It surprised her that she didn't have to fake that emotion. "I recently secured a new assignment."

"Oh, really. What can you tell us about that?"

"I'll be heading to Yellowstone and studying wolves. I've always been fascinated by them and their community. They're glorious creatures. I'm amazed by how their population has grown, but they face similar problems as the gorilla. They are a misunderstood species and are often hunted for sport. I'm looking forward to spending some time understanding their family life. How they communicate with each other and the other animals in the wild. I'm very excited about it. While I'll miss the gorillas, it's time for me to move on to something else."

"When do you start?"

"As soon as I get back," Kirby said. "There was an opening and while I thought about taking some time off, I believe my team would want me to honor them by continuing the work we were all so passionate about. You see, it was never only about gorillas. I turned what was supposed to be a three-year study into five. I don't regret that decision. I've loved every second of my time here, but my desire has always been to study all communal species, with a special focus on endangered species. Understanding how they function as a group helps us keep them around."

"Yellowstone and the wolves are lucky to have you. Is there a website or a place where people can follow your work?" Sally asked.

"Absolutely. The foundation is called Save the Gray Wolf. I will be updating my section of the site regularly."

"That's wonderful. Perhaps we can do a follow-up interview after you get settled at Yellowstone."

"I'd love that," Kirby said. "I also hope that you will continue to follow the story here because I don't believe it's over. I only wish I could have done more, but I'm being forced to leave."

"Thank you so much for taking the time to sit down with me today and I look forward to seeing you back in the States." Sally turned toward the camera and ended the interview. She unhooked her mic and set her notebook on the floor by her feet. "The first interview will air tomorrow. The second one the next day unless I'm told otherwise."

Kirby handed the mic to one of Sally's crew. "Please stay safe while you're here."

"I've got good people protecting me. Don't you worry." Sally rose. "I'll be in touch."

Kirby stood, stretching out her back.

"You did great." Wyatt appeared at her side, resting his hand on her forearm.

"You really think they will come after me in the States?" she asked. "I feel like we've barely poked the bear."

"We all but said the ambassador is doing something nefarious. We mentioned guns and drugs. You aren't going to stop talking about it at every turn. You even said you're going to put it in your book. They are going to want to shut you up before you get a chance to do that."

She shivered. "That doesn't make me feel better."

"Come on. We've got a long plane ride home."

Home. For five years, the Congo had been that place. Not the States.

"My parents have been freaking out. My mom was crying on the phone this morning, telling me this is no place for a lady. She believes I'm too old to be doing this and possibly my chance at finding a decent man to build a family with has passed me by. My dad demanded I return to Utah. It wasn't a request. It was more of a command."

"My head is exploding. I'm not sure how to respond to any of that. Did they even ask how you were holding up?"

"Not really. My father did ask if you were helping at all."

Wyatt cocked his head. "And what did you tell him?"

"That I hired your organization to get to the bottom of what was going on and you want to know what his response was?"

"I'm scared to even ask."

She scoffed. "He was glad that a man was taking care of things, but he wasn't sure a coward like you was the person for the job." She shook her head. "That's when I informed him that I had a new gig in Yellowstone and I'd come visit when I could, but I wasn't sure when."

"I'm not sure I want to go to Utah when you do." Wyatt wrapped a protective arm around her and guided her toward the lobby of the hotel. "The more you tell me about your parents, the more I don't want to meet them."

"I don't think they like me, so what difference does it make." She'd stopped wanting to please her parents the day she broke up with her ex-boyfriend. It had been the most freeing experience of her life. "I'm a trophy to them. Something they bring out to show off to their friends when I come home to visit. I'm a possession, not a person."

"That makes me sad."

"I've accepted it. I love them because they're my parents, but I don't live my life for them." She paused and stared up into Wyatt's kind, dark eyes. "I have to live for me, but I'm learning to like the idea that I can share it with someone else more permanently."

"Good, because I'm not going anywhere."

She had no idea what the future held, except that there was room for Wyatt in her heart.

CHAPTER 13

SLOWLY, Wyatt stepped from the helicopter. He sucked in a deep breath, praying all he needed was a few minutes to ground himself, but he knew better. The nausea spread from the pit of his gut up to the center of his throat and through the rest of his body like a raging wildfire. His muscles turned to rubber, barely able to hold his weight.

"I'll get you some water," Booker said softly.

Thank God for Booker and the rest of his team. Gunn, Hunter, and Xavier all knew not to make a huge deal of what was about to happen. No one, not even Wyatt, knew if this would be a minor attack or the one that put Wyatt down for days. Only, Wyatt had a bad feeling about this one. It had been inching up on him for the last hour. It had started with a dull ache in the back of his skull. Three short jabs to his temples had already occurred. Ice-pick migraines. Fucking good description for that pain. It was four or five seconds of pure hell. Sometimes they led to a different kind of headache; other times they didn't.

But once the nausea came and the vision went, Wyatt was fucked.

Hunter came up on one side and Xavier on the other as they strolled alongside him across the tarmac toward the hangar where Gunn had taken off to, most likely to make sure Wyatt had a chair to sit in.

"What can I do?" Kirby asked, trying unsuccessfully to wedge herself between Gunn and Wyatt. "Is it really bad this time?"

Wyatt opened his mouth, but he couldn't answer. The words wouldn't come. But he also didn't want her anywhere near him, especially since he thought he might fall over every time he lifted his foot. "You can get my bag," he managed.

"And you could bring the Jeep around," Hunter said. "Booker has the keys."

"You can do that. I'll stay with Wyatt." Kirby took his arm.

"Don't." He jerked it away, which turned out to be a huge mistake as he stumbled to the right, bumping into Xavier, who thankfully didn't grab him, but used his body to ensure Wyatt didn't fall flat on his face.

"I'll help you." Hunter placed his hand on Kirby's

back. "Come on. There's a lot of gear that needs to be packed up."

"I'm staying with Wyatt," Kirby said with a defiant tone. "He needs my—"

"Please, Kirby. Not here." Wyatt did his best to hold her gaze and he took a few more tentative steps.

"You can take care of him at home," Hunter whispered just loud enough for Wyatt to hear as Hunter whisked her away.

"I hated doing that." Wyatt swallowed the bile that bubbled from his stomach. "But I don't want the attention."

"Here comes Booker with water. Where's your medication?" Xavier asked.

"Booker always carries extra in case I can't get to it in time." Wyatt knew his words were slurred and he probably walked like a drunken sailor. He didn't hide his condition from anyone, but his pride still got in the way.

"Here you go." Booker handed him two pills and an ice-cold aqua bottle.

Gunn had set up a circle of chairs to make it appear as though they were having an after-action chat.

Wyatt would be lost without these men. They were his family in the truest sense of the word. He lowered himself into the chair, downed the pills in one swallow, and placed the cold bottle on his neck.

He couldn't see shit and the fucking room moved as if he were in the roughest of seas. He worried he might vomit. This kind of migraine could bring up his biggest nightmare.

The Brotherhood Protectors might have to let him out of his contract.

Or put him behind a desk, rendering him fucking useless.

"Dumb as fuck question, but how far am I from the bathroom?" Wyatt pressed his hands on his knees and breathed through the pain that felt like someone was raging a war inside his head.

"Fifteen paces to the left," Booker said.

"Take me there, now." Wyatt went to stand but ended up landing on his ass. "Fuck."

Booker and Xavier lifted him to his feet.

He coughed and gagged while they dragged him across the hangar, his pride dangling in the air. The sharp jabs shot across his brain like a cattle prod. He was toast. "Call the doctor."

∽

"Why didn't you tell me he was still suffering this badly? Why didn't he tell me?" Kirby paced in the waiting room of the Brotherhood Protectors' medical facility, glaring at Booker.

"Because he hasn't been getting them very often

and certainly not like this." Booker stuffed his hands in his pockets and lowered his head. "He's only had two since we got here. The last one was mild. Lasting only a few minutes. Barely a migraine at all."

"When was it?"

"The day you got here."

"And before that?" Kirby asked.

"While we were still at Brighter Days Rehab Ranch. But over the course of time, they were becoming less frequent and more mild. Nothing like what happened today." Booker rubbed the back of his neck and glanced toward the ceiling. "He'd been improving. The last scans showed there was no permanent damage from the brain injury. The doctors had said with time, everything else should fall into place and gave him the thumbs-up to go back to work with monitoring of the migraines."

"He's always pushed himself too hard and you and the rest of the guys don't do him any favors by trying to hide it."

Booker's face hardened. His lips drew into a tight line. "You're way out of line, Kirby."

"Am I?" She shook her head. "Maybe if you had helped him across the tarmac instead of letting him walk—"

"Stop right there," Booker said. "Wyatt knows his body. He understands his condition. What he can and can't do. He doesn't want to be coddled or have unnecessary attention placed on what was happening. I know you care about him, but so do I, and I'm the one who's responsible for him having the fucking brain injury in the first place, so don't come in here and start telling me how to deal with it or him."

Callie strolled into the waiting area carrying a tray of coffee. "Lower your voices. I could hear you all the way down the hall." She handed a mug to each of them. "Bickering about what happened isn't helping Wyatt. Besides, no one could have prevented it, including Wyatt. Migraines happen and we all know the doctors told him this could be part of his new normal for the rest of his life. Our job now is to support him and help him through this because the Brotherhood Protectors could either put him behind a desk or completely end his career."

Booker raked a hand across his head, turned, and let out an audible groan.

"It's not your fault." Callie placed a hand on Booker's shoulder.

"Isn't it though?"

"The crash was an accident." Kirby blinked out a tear. "I'm sorry if you ever for one second believed I blamed you."

"I blame myself," Booker whispered. "Good men died that day and while I'm grateful Wyatt and the rest of this team and others didn't, I can't stop wondering if I'd only done—"

"Stop that," Callie commanded. "Wyatt doesn't need this bullshit and I don't want to hear it."

Kirby stepped in front of Booker. "I was only trying to understand because Wyatt has chosen to downplay his condition."

"He wasn't doing that," Callie said. "The doctors wouldn't have let him come here and go on missions if he wasn't ready. Let's hope this was a temporary setback and there's nothing else going on." She squeezed Kirby's shoulder.

"I've let so many years go by living my life in fear of loving anyone. Of being committed to anything other than my work because people have only let me down and here I've done the same thing to Wyatt. I should have been more engaged in his recovery instead of going back to be with my gorillas."

"No." Callie gave her a weak smile. "You and Wyatt had a lot of things to work out both professionally and personally. Don't beat yourself up about something you weren't ready for. You're here now, by his side. That's what matters."

Deep down, Kirby knew Callie was right. It hadn't been until the crash that nearly took Wyatt's life that she realized Wyatt was more than a friend with benefits, but her grant had been renewed so she could write her book. That was something she couldn't give up and Wyatt had kept her at arm's length after the accident. At the time she believed it was because he wanted to keep things exactly the way they were, not to mention he needed to focus on his recovery.

She'd accepted that reality and continued on her path, loving him from a distance. She entrenched herself in her work, giving it everything she had, ignoring what she really wanted.

Wyatt.

Even after telling him she loved him, she still wanted to focus on her career. She viewed working with the wolves as temporary while they caught Kofi and the rest of the smugglers, figuring something else would come along.

However, after today, she knew her place was with Wyatt. What that future looked like, she didn't know, but she needed to find out.

The sliding doors opened and Wyatt's doctor entered the waiting room. She was a petite older woman with white hair and dark glasses. She carried a clipboard and wore a warm smile. "Hello," she said. "Good to see you, Booker. Callie."

"Hey, Doctor Willow." Booker nodded. "This is Kirby Carrington."

"Wyatt's told me a little about you." Doctor Willow tucked her clipboard under her arm and held out her hand. "Please, will everyone call me Anita."

"It's nice to meet you, Anita." Kirby swallowed. "How's Wyatt?"

"He's doing much better and is asking for you," Anita said. "I'm sending him home with a minor change in his medication. He can leave when I finish the paperwork and Booker brings the car around. Wyatt can't drive for twenty-four hours. After that, he can go back to the office, but I'm restricting his workload until I get the CT scan results back."

"That's going to piss him off," Booker said.

"Trust me, he let me know his feelings on that one." Anita laughed. "But since he hasn't had an episode like this one in over eight months and he's still struggling with finding the right words and a little vertigo, I want to be cautious."

"Thanks, Doc." Booker nodded. "Come on, Callie. Let's get the Jeep so Kirby can take him home."

"This might be helpful." Anita took her clipboard and handed a packet to Kirby.

"What's this?"

"Information on Wyatt's condition and migraines. It will help you understand what could be triggering them. I know Wyatt has been experimenting lately on what might or might not be causing some of them, which is fine. But I'm not always sure he's documenting them." Anita turned and the sliding doors opened. "He says he is and so far, nothing has set him off except for one day of flying and now this, but there is no pattern. That's a concern for me."

"Are you sure it will be okay for him to go to the office in a day?" Kirby asked. "Because he'll go and work his ass off if you tell him he can."

"I wouldn't give him the green light if I thought

otherwise. I don't want him flying, firing a weapon, or doing anything too strenuous. My only other concern is all his computer screens, but he knows to dim them, take breaks, and to shut down at the first sign of symptoms."

"Does he follow your instructions?" Kirby didn't know shit about Wyatt and that made her feel like a shitty girlfriend.

"I'd say about ninety-five percent of the time." Anita paused in front of a closed door. "Where he tends to fall off the rails is understanding that just because this could change the course of his life, it's not career-ending."

"What do you mean?"

"He truly thinks that if I pull him off active duty with the Brotherhood Protectors, his life is essentially over. But it's not. Going on missions is only one aspect of the job. His skill set is unique, and Stone needs his computer savvy and intelligence background. He's vital to this operation. Maybe you can help him understand that."

"Are you saying that he won't be able to—"

"I have no idea. Not until I read the CT scan. We need to see how he recovers from this episode and if he has more. Time will be the judge, but if I'm being honest, the stress of the missions, the flying, and some other factors may be triggers that are too great and I fear that is what is best for him," Anita said. "I might be overstepping my role as his doctor, but I can tell he has deep feelings. His face lit up like a Christmas tree when he told me about you. He will need all the love and support he can get."

"It will kill him if he can't work missions."

Anita curled her fingers around Kirby's forearm. "Even if I have to pull him from active protection detail, he'll still be on the team and working missions. It will just be in a different role. But he'll need someone besides me, Stone, or even Booker telling him that. He won't hear it from us. But he might hear it from the woman who loves him." Anita arched a brow.

"I don't have the first clue as to how to do that."

"My advice would be to lift him up, showing him all the things he's good at, and not to let him feel sorry for himself if I hand down the worst-case scenario."

"That's going to be easier said than done."

"I have faith in you," Anita said. "He's waiting for you to take him home. I'll get the wheelchair. You tell him that's the only way he's getting out of this joint."

Kirby put on her best smile and opened the door.

"You are a sight for sore eyes." Wyatt held up two fingers. "And I get to see two of you."

"That's not funny." She chuckled. "Booker's bringing your Jeep around. As soon as Doctor Willow comes back with the—"

"I can walk on my own two feet." He swung his

legs to the side of the bed and gripped the mattress. "On second thought, I'll wait."

"Good decision." She eased onto the gurney, rested her hand on his thigh, and squeezed. "You scared me today."

"It's not a big deal."

"Not true," Kirby said. "I need you to promise me that you will be honest about your symptoms."

"I'm never not."

"With your team," she said with a little more frustration laced to her words than intended. "I respect they are your brothers and I would never stand in the way of that bond. But I'm the one sleeping in your bed, not them. I need you to tell me what you need and when."

He took her hand and kissed her palm. "I can do that."

She jerked her head back. "You didn't do that today. You pushed me away."

"Because I was at work and you're our client. I needed to separate my personal life from my work life."

"I can live with that, but had I known the desired protocol, I would have followed it and my feelings wouldn't have been hurt."

"Fair enough."

"Here comes the doctor with your wheels," Kirby said. "Let's get you home. I'll make you meatballs and spaghetti for dinner."

"And chocolate chip cookies for dessert? You make the best."

"Absolutely not," she said. "Chocolate is a trigger."

"Since when did you become an expert on migraines?"

She laughed. "I spent the last three hours reading up on them and your doctor gave me an entire packet on your condition. You can't hide shit from me now."

"Nothing worse than having all the women in my life gang up on me."

"I can make you peanut butter ones, but you're spending the rest of the day in bed."

"Oh. I can think of a few things we can do to kill some time."

She rolled her eyes. "You need brain rest and that means doing absolutely nothing, including physical exertion."

"I can just lie there."

"Not happening," she said. "But I'll make it up to you when you're feeling better. Now get your ass in that wheelchair so I can go home and read up on migraines and wolves." She took him by the elbow and eased him into the chair. Standing behind it, she rolled him into the hallway, pausing when she saw Hunter leaning against the wall. "What are you doing here?"

"I'm your new protection detail." Hunter smiled. "At least until that asshole gets a clean bill of health."

Wyatt groaned. "Fucking wonderful."

"She starts work with the wolves tomorrow," Hunter said. "She can't go out there alone and with you out of commission, someone needs to be there. I drew the short straw."

"I'm insulted," Kirby said with a short laugh. "Hunter helping me with wolves. That's ironic."

CHAPTER 14

Wyatt wiggled his fingers over the keyboard and stared at the main computer screen. It had been three days since his episode and he'd yet to get a decent night's sleep. The symptoms from his last migraine still lingered. The brain fog had yet to lift and he'd had to dim the brightness on his screens in fear of it affecting his vision. He reached for his second cup of coffee. Normally, he limited himself to one cup a day. The doctors told him that while caffeine could help ward off migraines when symptoms arose, it could also cause one, so he didn't want to risk it by having too much.

However, lack of sleep was making it hard to focus, a side effect from the brain injury.

He double-checked the status of Kofi and his known associates. So far, there had been no known movement, and Wyatt's patience had run thin. He knew he needed to give it time. Kofi wasn't a stupid man. He wouldn't come racing into the United States without a plan.

But what scared Wyatt the most was that if he were Kofi, he wouldn't come at all. He'd hire someone to do his dirty work. That meant Wyatt didn't know who was coming.

He snagged his cell and quickly shot off a message to Ridley, hoping he'd have some information to report. He hated that he wasn't the one out in the trenches with Kirby while she studied the wolves. Yesterday, Booker had taken that role. Today it was Xavier. Tomorrow, Gunn. It would continue to rotate until he got full clearance.

Knock. Knock.

Wyatt swiveled. "Hey, Stone, what brings you by this morning?"

"Wanted to get an update on the Kirby case." Stone waved a file in the air. "And let you know the doctor sent her report."

It was standard for Stone to receive the medical report, but only after Wyatt had gotten it first. And Stone not once showed up in his office to discuss it, which made Wyatt more than a little nervous, especially because of that last migraine. He rested his elbows on his desk, clasped his hands together, and braced himself for the worst. "Doctor Willow hasn't called me and I don't go back to see her until the end of the week."

"I know, but I was at the medical facility this morning and I had asked her to give me the information ahead of you anyway."

"I don't like the direction this is going already."

"Let's table that for a second and start with the worst news, in my opinion," Stone said. "The local government made an arrest in the murders of Kirby's teammates."

"Why are you scowling?" Wyatt asked.

"Because it wasn't Kofi. Some small group is screaming that they are innocent, but the ambassador is signing off on this, stating it's over. Justice is being served. He wants Sally to come back and do a wrap-up piece, so they can put the whole sordid mess behind them."

"That's bullshit, especially when Kofi has gone AWOL. For all we know, he's slipped into the country."

"I'm not going to argue that point," Stone said. "I spoke with Sally; she will ignore the ambassador for now, buying us a little time."

"What about the Department of Defense? The DEA?" Wyatt lifted his cell. "I haven't heard anything from Ridley in a while."

"Our government isn't making a statement at this time and they aren't happy about the ambassador. I'm sure that's why we haven't heard from Ridley," Stone said. "But let me know as soon as you do, okay?"

Wyatt nodded. "Anything else regarding Kirby and the case?"

"Not at this time."

"Then I'd like to dive right into what you and the good doctor discussed," Wyatt said.

"Before I get into Anita's report, I want to go over why I hired you."

Wyatt leaned back, dropping his hands to his lap, resisting the urge to fold his arms across his chest. This change in topic felt like a deflection and that drove him crazy. "I came as part of a package deal."

"That's only partly true," Stone said. "When Booker first discussed an aviation branch of the Brotherhood Protectors with Hank and me, we were more than intrigued. However, your file stuck out as something uniquely different."

"I'm no more special than anyone else on this team."

"I don't disagree. Everyone brings something to the table," Stone said. "However, your degree in cyber operations and your career with the Navy in communications, intelligence, and being a SEAL team leader is a skill set that we wanted to use outside the scope of the aviation unit."

"That was mentioned in my interview." Wyatt nodded.

"You told me before that you know Darius Ford, who works in our Colorado branch."

"We've crossed paths a time or two. He's a good man and a genius."

"I think your IQ is higher than his." Stone laughed. "We want you to do what he does in Colorado for us here in Yellowstone."

"Is that because of what my medical report states? Or because of where you need me?" Wyatt asked. "And doesn't Darius' unit run a training facility?"

"He does. We send everyone through Colorado right now, but I'd like to run certain things right here. I have the men to do it. What I don't have is a good leader and someone who has the computer chops to run cyber internally. I constantly have to send that work to Darius or another man in Montana. I'd like you to head it up here."

"Let me get this straight." Wyatt threaded his fingers through his hair. "You want me to create some kind of high-level training program as well as be in charge of all the Yellowstone Brotherhood Protector cyber issues."

"In a nutshell, yes." Stone nodded.

"You didn't answer my very first question." Wyatt pointed to the folder. "Am I being pulled from active duty? Did my latest CT scan show something unusual?"

"There has been no change in the imaging. No new swelling or brain bleeds. However, Anita is recommending that we take you out of the rotation for six months. She feels we might have rushed it.

Not to mention that you may suffer from these types of attacks for the rest of your life." Stone leaned forward, tapping his fingers on the folder. "You are a valuable asset to this organization and I want to use you in the best, most productive capacity. I don't want to lose you."

"What about Kirby's case?"

"That depends on how you feel and how it plays out, but she's allowing you to follow through with it." Stone raised his hand. "As long as it doesn't require you to get on an aircraft and it's the only mission you're physically active on."

Wyatt did his best to digest the information. "What happens after six months?"

"Full physical and another scan, but she believes you're not going to get any better than where you are now and that I'd be crazy to let you go on another mission," Stone said. "It doesn't mean you can't be deployed with the team in a more stabilized role or that we can't have this discussion again, but I'd rather discuss my other offer." He lowered his chin. "We have five men coming in next month that were at the ranch with you."

"The men in the other helicopter crash the day Booker's went down."

"Yes," Stone said. "They will need training, assessments, and placements based on their past experiences. Not to mention the current caseload and the intelligence and communication support they all need that we must hire out or send elsewhere. I need you right here doing what you do best."

Wyatt pinched the bridge of his nose. For the first part of his life he'd been called a geek. A brain. Girls only spoke to him when they wanted help with their homework. He dreamed about being something other than the smart one in his group. He wanted to be the brawn. To be cool. Becoming a SEAL had given him something he had always thought had been unattainable.

Having that stripped away felt as though someone was taking away his manhood.

Deep down, he knew that wasn't true, but it didn't change the facts.

He was being decommissioned and that sucked.

But what was the alternative? Age and perhaps a little wisdom inched into his brain. He'd be a fool to walk away.

"All right. I'll take the position," he said. His entire life had been a challenge and he'd risen to every single one. This shouldn't be any different.

"You'll be bombarded with paperwork tomorrow and there will be a meeting with me and Hank at eight sharp. You'll still be the front man for Kirby's case, but until something happens, it will up to the rest of your team to run protection detail."

"I understand." Wyatt stood and stretched out his arm. "I won't let you down."

"I know you won't." Stone strolled out of the

office, leaving Wyatt to his thoughts, which quickly went down a strange and unexpected rabbit hole.

Kirby.

A normal life filled with dinners and dare he think it.

Children.

The only time they'd ever discussed the topic had been the first time they went without birth control. He swallowed. Hard.

He once told Booker that everything happened for a reason. He didn't actually believe it at the time. It had been his gallant effort in helping Booker overcome the shock of their careers ending and making the shift to the Brotherhood Protectors.

But perhaps it was true.

"Hey," a familiar and welcomed voice echoed in his office.

He swiveled in his chair and smiled. "I didn't expect to see you here this early."

Kirby shrugged. "The wolves aren't cooperating and I thought I'd come see if you're free for lunch." She held up a basket of goodies. "I brought sandwiches, chips, and boring water."

"Sounds perfect," he said. "Why don't we take it outside? It's above forty out. There are picnic benches around back." He shut down his system, stood, and grabbed his jacket. "Are you enjoying your new post?"

"Truth?"

"Yes." He took the basket from her hands and strolled down the corridor. "But now I'm scared you don't like it here."

"It's an adjustment," she said. "Wolves are very different from gorillas. While they are social with each other, I worry I'm never going to get as close to them as I did with Tav and his group."

"Give it time. I'm sure it will happen." He pushed open the door and pulled out his shades. Sun still killed his eyes, making his head want to hide under the blanket.

"How are you feeling?"

"About eighty-five percent." He decided honesty needed to be his friend, especially because he wanted things between him and Kirby to work. "I still have a headache and I can only spend about forty minutes at the computer, which is frustrating as hell. But at least I can see straight, and the vertigo is gone." He set the basket on the table and pulled out a sandwich. "You should know I've been put on desk duty for a while with the exception of working your case when it comes to a showdown."

She tilted her head. "I know that's not what you wanted to hear."

"I'm not thrilled, but I'm going to make the best of it. This is an opportunity and I love my team."

"Who are you and what have you done with my boyfriend?"

He laughed. "I'm trying to tell myself it's not the

end of the world. That there's still a place here for me. That I'm not irrelevant."

She reached across the table and palmed his face. "I understand how important your work is to you and that these men are your family. I wish I had that."

"You do," he said.

Tears filled her beautiful eyes. "I spoke to my father this morning. It didn't go well."

"What happened?"

"He doesn't understand why I went from one job right to the next or why I won't come home, so I told him."

Wyatt arched a brow. "What exactly did you say?"

"That I can't go back to a place where people pretend and if he and Mom aren't willing to deal with their problems, then I won't be a part of it. That all I want is for them to be real with each other or at the very least, with me. I went on to say that if he can't be supportive of me and my career, then we don't have much of a relationship."

"I can't imagine that went over well."

She let out a dry laugh. "He told me I had no idea what I was talking about when it came to him and my mom. And where my life was concerned, he told me to stop being so selfish. That all I've ever done since college is make my mom worry and cry. When I got off the phone with him, I called my mother and told her the same thing and do you know what she told me?"

"I can't wait to hear this."

Kirby swiped her wet cheeks. "She told me to grow up and stop running."

"This is none of my business, but have your parents ever considered it's them you're running from?"

"Oh, trust me, that's what I told her and her response was that her marriage was none of my business and that maybe if I had a real man in my life, I'd understand what a relationship was all about. I proceeded to tell her about you and she laughed. She told me if you actually cared about me, you wouldn't sit around and wait for me to stop playing with my animals. That you'd insist on me returning to the States and asking my dad for my hand in marriage. I tried to convince her that I wouldn't bring you around to meet them because I was ashamed of them, but she insisted either it was the other way around or that you were a loser. And she reminded me that I screwed up my only real relationship and killed her grandchild."

"Jesus. She actually said that to you?"

Kirby nodded.

Wyatt moved to the other side of the picnic table and wrapped his arm around Kirby. "That's not what you did."

"I know that, but it doesn't take the sting away."

He pressed his lips against her temple.

She rested her head on his shoulder. "I ended the

call by telling my mom that I loved her, but I couldn't communicate with her or have a relationship with her anymore unless she was willing to do two things. The first one is stop pretending and the second is to forgive me for doing something I needed to do for myself. She told she could never forgive me and hung up on me."

"I'm so sorry."

"So am I, but I'm done. I'm not going to play this game anymore. They are both so miserable and while I know I haven't been the greatest daughter in the world, it kills me that they expected me to either stay with a man who cheated on me, as if that's the norm. Or have a baby that would have been in a tug-of-war its entire life." She glanced up, catching his gaze. "They got married because of me and I think they have both resented that decision and me ever since."

"Bringing this up is really shitty timing, but the topic of conversation is leading me there." Wyatt ran his finger across her cheek. "I get it will be at least a week before we'll know, but we did go without birth control."

"Wyatt—"

He pressed his finger over her lips.

"Coming to terms with the fact my career will most likely have to shift permanently with the Brotherhood Protectors into more of a desk job than a missions position at first made my blood boil. But as

Stone and I discussed my role, it made me rethink what I wanted my life to look like."

"I don't understand."

"I love you so much, Kirby. I have for a long time. I don't know why I fought it. But I think you know what kind of man I am and I would never hurt you intentionally. I'm not a cheater."

"I know that."

"I've never given much thought to having a family. My career was all I ever cared about until I met you. Slowly, you've changed how I view the world and I find myself thinking about things like getting married and having kids."

"You're a sweet man, but don't say things just because—"

He hushed her with a kiss. "Whether or not you are pregnant doesn't change the way I feel. And this isn't something that happened overnight. The shift came after the crash, when I knew for sure that I loved you. I was just too afraid you'd reject me."

"It's hard for me to believe that you're afraid of anything. That is until I saw the terror in your eyes when we got on that airplane." She laughed. "But being pregnant again is something that horrifies me. That was the worst experience in my life."

"I can't even imagine what you went through, but you had no support system. And if the time isn't right, we'll deal with it."

She jerked her head back. "You're serious, aren't you?"

"I don't want to force you into something you're not ready for and it's your body." He brushed her hair from her face. "I'm telling you what I can see in our future and I hope it's a future you might be able to see someday too."

"I love you, Wyatt. I'm just scared. I had a pretty crappy childhood when I go back and examine it. What if I'm a shitty mom?"

He took her chin with his thumb and forefinger. "You'll make a wonderful mother. It's me you'll have to worry about in the parenting department."

"Why's that?"

"Because I'm just a big kid myself and I will spoil them rotten." He winked.

Playfully, she slapped his shoulder and sighed. "Can we table this discussion until we know?"

"Of course."

"How did I get so lucky have found someone like you?" she asked.

"Maybe it's because we were friends first."

"We had sex before you even got my name right."

He burst out laughing, remembering he had thought her name was Riley the entire night. "It was loud in that bar and you made fun of me, calling me Wyatt Earp."

"You do look like a cowboy. Even more so now that you live in Yellowstone."

"I guess I need to buy a Stetson." While not everything in his life was perfect, things were certainly looking up.

Now all they had to do was catch Kofi and he'd be able to rest easy.

CHAPTER 15

Kirby blew out a puff of air and stared between the stick and the directions. She wasn't even sure if she was late for her period. She didn't track it because she never needed to. Besides, she hadn't been regular since she started menstruating at fourteen.

But it had been two weeks since she and Wyatt had unprotected sex the first time.

There had been two other times they failed to reach for the condom. She didn't know if they both figured why bother or if she was secretly trying to get pregnant and he was doing the same thing.

The timing would suck. He was struggling—whether he wanted to admit it or not—with his new position, and she'd started a new job that was still considered temporary. She'd filed all the necessary paperwork to make it a more permanent gig, but that could take a few months, and even then, she could always be turned down.

That would suck. She wanted to stay in Yellowstone, and not only for the wolves.

"Kirby? Where are you?" Wyatt's voice rattled through the wood door.

"In the bathroom." She stared at the directions. Five more minutes. Shit. "I'll be out shortly." This was going to be the longest few minutes in her entire life. She tapped her fingers against the sink and leaned closer to the mirror. When she opened her eyes this morning, her stomach felt like it had consumed an entire bottle of spoiled milk. She hadn't thought anything of it until her feet hit the floor, she stood, and the room spun around her as if she'd been on one of those crazy rides at the carnival where its sole purpose was to make you puke.

However, as soon as she had her shower, a little food, and some coffee, those feelings disappeared, and they hadn't returned. But it put the baby thought in the back of her mind for the rest of the day.

"Everything alright in there?" Wyatt called.

"Just washing the grim of Yellowstone off my face and from under my nails." She glanced at her watch. Two more minutes. Well, maybe the stupid test would have already done its thing. She snagged it from the back of the toilet and lifted it toward the light. She blinked. Her heart dropped to her toes and bounced to her throat like a basketball.

"Holy fuck," she mumbled. "Pregnant." She let out a long breath. A slew of mixed emotions raced through her body. If there was anyone she wanted to start a family with, it was Wyatt. He'd made his feelings crystal clear in the sense he'd support her decision no matter what she wanted. She lowered the toilet seat and sat. Having a child hadn't been part of her plan. Her parents were right that she'd been running her entire life. Fear kept her from forming attachments to people.

She'd made a connection with Wyatt and she knew without a shadow of a doubt that their love was real. But was it enough and were they ready?

Knock. Knock.

"I'm starting to worry about you in there," he said.

Not telling him would be a mistake. She demanded the truth from him, so how could she give him anything less.

She shouldn't have taken the fucking test. No way would she be able to walk out of the bathroom and look him in the eye and keep this to herself. It wouldn't be fair. She rose and smoothed down the front of her jeans. Gripping the knob, she pushed open the door. "Hey, you," she managed with a weak smile. "How was your day?"

"Wasn't the worst, but I hate meetings and paperwork and this new position is going to require a lot of that. And the rest of the aviation crew is coming in a couple of weeks. The preparation for that is more than I expected. I also spoke to Ridley." Wyatt wrapped his arms around her waist and tugged her close to his chest. "He thinks he might have a line on Kofi and a few of his men. The ambassador came to the US yesterday. He believes Kofi might have hitched a ride. Ridley landed Stateside about an hour ago."

"How is that possible? Is he sure?" She swallowed her beating heart. Part of her believed telling Wyatt about the baby would add to his stress, which was the last thing he needed while he was still dealing with the fallout from his last episode.

"He's not positive, but it was a last-minute trip and the ambassador did it without much fanfare. Actually, it was quite secretive and in a private charter." Wyatt pressed his lips over her mouth. "I've asked Booker to come over. He'll be here in a half hour with Callie. We need to discuss a plan because if the intel that Ridley gave us is accurate, Kofi could already be in the area." He ran his thumb across her cheek. "What's wrong?"

"Nothing."

"Bullshit. Something was troubling you before I told you about the ambassador and Kofi," Wyatt said. "We made a promise that we weren't going to keep things from each other so I'm asking nicely for you to please tell me."

"You better sit down for this."

"Sounds serious."

"It is." She took him by the hand and led him into the main room. "Want a beer or something?"

"Why not." He ducked his head into the fridge and pulled out two.

She shook her head.

He arched a brow.

Most of her adult life, she enjoyed an adult beverage or two to wind down from a long day. It wasn't every night, but it was rare she turned one down.

Wyatt leaned against the counter and swigged. "You've got my full attention."

"I want you to know that I'm not unhappy about this or us; it's just that I'm not exactly sure how I feel considering the conversation I had with my parents."

He set his beer on the counter and strolled to where she'd perched herself on the stool in front of the island. He wiped away the tear that had dribbled down her cheek. "You can always open the door to your parents. They might not want to cut you out of their lives any more than you really want to do that to them. After we deal with Kofi and get this new team settled, we can take a trip and begin to mend fences, that is if you want, but I think if they see the kind of person you've become and understand that all you want is for them to be real with you, things will eventually work themselves out."

"I love how you are always so willing to support

me and let me deal with things slowly. You've never once pressured me."

"You've been the same way with me. It's why we've worked for so long." He pulled out a stool. "Are you worried because we've defined our relationship everything will change?"

"Yes," she admitted. "But it's so much more because things have changed." She sucked in a deep breath of courage. "I took a home test."

"A home test for what?"

"You know, one of those things a woman pees on that tells her if she needs to make an appointment with a doctor to confirm her suspicions." Jesus. She'd never been the kind of person who didn't know how to spit things out, but she couldn't bring herself to simply say the words. It made it real and there was no running from that.

"Kirby, my brain isn't firing on all cylinders currently. I might have the IQ of a genius, but right now, it physically hurts to think to..." His words trailed off and his eyes grew wide with shock. His gaze lowered to her midsection and then snapped back up to meet her stare. "A pregnancy test?"

She nodded. "It was positive."

He raked a hand across the top of his head. "Not unhappy, but you didn't say happy."

"It's a lot to take in considering everything we've been through and what's going on with Kofi."

"Agreed, but we knew it could happen since we

didn't use birth control." He wiggled his fingers. "At least three times that I have counted."

"You're keeping score?" She let out a nervous laugh.

"No, but we didn't discuss it after the fact and it's like playing Russian roulette." He took her hand, kissing the palm. "I have given this a fair amount of thought and I told you that I will stand by you."

"You have, but that doesn't exactly tell me how you feel, and before you go into your spiel about my body, my decision—which I totally appreciate—we're not kids. We're not in a friends-with-benefits situation anymore. I want to know what your thoughts and feelings are and I want you to be honest."

"That certainly is a reasonable request." He leaned in, pressing his mouth over hers in a warm, tender kiss. "I love you and I want a life with you. That includes children. Yes, I would love to have this baby with you, but if you're not ready or don't believe we are—"

"Is anyone ever ready to be parents?"

He chuckled. "Probably not. The thought is kind of terrifying."

She took his hand and placed it over her stomach. "I'm scared, but I want to do this."

"Then it's settled." He smiled like a kid at Christmas.

"Please don't be mad, but I don't want to tell anyone yet. Too much is going on and too many things could go wrong, like I could have a miscarriage."

He palmed her face. "Don't think negatively."

"I'm being realistic."

"We don't have to say anything to anyone for now. Besides, I'm not prepared for the razzing I'm going to get from my team."

"That's what you're worried about?"

"Oh, hell yes," he said. "One razzing at a time. If Booker grew a pair, he proposed to Callie when he got home. I saw the ring. We're all going to have fun giving that man shit for weeks. I'm more than happy to let that die down… Do you want to get married?"

She jerked her head back. "Wyatt Harrison Bixby, are you proposing to me?"

"I'm horrible at being romantic and I should go out and buy you a ring and do it proper and all."

"I don't want me being pregnant to be the reason we get married."

"Okay, but is it something you'd consider?" He arched a brow.

"Yes, but don't you dare get all weird on me. It's a piece of paper. We don't need it to be a family." If there was one thing she believed wholeheartedly, it was that. "We love each other, that's enough."

"Except this place is too damn small. We'll have to find a bigger place. I'll start looking tomorrow."

She closed her eyes and shook her head. "Relax,

cowboy. It will be months before we need that. Let's enjoy where we are."

He glanced at his watch. "Speaking of that. Callie and Booker will be here in fifteen. I need to go start the grill. They are bringing a salad."

"I better go dispose of the baby evidence and get myself ready." She hopped off the stool, took two steps, and glanced over her shoulder. "You're not going to let me go see my wolves tomorrow, are you?"

"Until this is over, you are glued to my hip and for the record, that has nothing to do with you being pregnant."

"I don't believe that for a second." But she wasn't about to argue with him about it either.

~

Wyatt stood in front of the sink and finished the last dish. Dinner had been mostly focused on Callie, Booker, and their glowing happiness. It was hard to razz a man who was so disgustingly in love, especially when Wyatt was sitting on his own joy. He wanted to scream it from the rooftops, but he would respect Kirby's wishes.

Booker would be pissed for all of five seconds, but he, of all people, would understand in the end.

"I can't believe Booker picked that out himself," Kirby said, holding up Callie's hand for the fifth time.

"He had some help." Wyatt set the plate in the cupboard. "I went with him to the jewelry store."

"So you've said a dozen of times." Callie smiled. "I'm going to need a maid of honor and I was hoping that Kirby would be willing."

"Oh my God. Seriously? Me? I'd be thrilled," Kirby asked. "When do you plan on getting married?"

"We haven't set a date yet." Booker stood behind Callie at the kitchen table, rubbing her shoulders. "We were thinking maybe April."

Wyatt took a seat next to Kirby and sipped his scotch. He hoped no one noticed Kirby drinking water the entire night. With the way his brain had been working, he still struggled to come up with the right words sometimes, and he was a shitty liar when it came to Booker.

"Or sooner. I don't want to wait too long."

Wyatt mentally counted the months. He didn't quite understand the exact workings of the female body when it came to babies, but he guessed Kirby would be about four or five months, so at least showing. A vision filled his mind and it took all his energy to suppress a smile. "We're here no matter when you decide to tie the knot."

"Good to know, because someone is going to have to make sure I get to the church on time."

Wyatt's cell buzzed. He pulled it from his back pocket. "Oh shit," he whispered.

"What is it?"

"Ben." He took Kirby's hand. "I'm sorry, he didn't make it." He handed her his phone, letting her read the message from his contacts at the hospital. "He died a few hours ago. He never did wake up. We won't ever be able to shed any light on what happened or why he got involved with smuggling."

Kirby set the phone on the table. "I don't wish ill will on anyone, but if he was involved, justice was served on some level."

Wyatt leaned over and kissed her temple.

Knock. Knock.

"Are you expecting anyone?" Booker asked.

"I am not." Wyatt stood and snagged his weapon from the cupboard where he kept it. No one ever showed up unannounced. At least none of his buddies ever did or anyone from the Brotherhood Protectors. It was an unwritten rule. Call or text; otherwise, you'd be greeted with a gun.

"Let me send a message to the team before you open that door," Booker said. "Might as well put everyone on alert."

"Sounds like a good plan." Wyatt inched through the family room. "I want everyone to go into my bedroom."

"Is that really necessary?" Kirby asked.

"Yes," Booker and Wyatt said in unison.

"Come on." Callie took Kirby by the hand. "Better safe than sorry."

"Hunter, Gunn, and Xavier are on their way over.

We can call them off if we need to." Booker checked his weapon. "Let's go see who decided to pay us a visit."

Wyatt nodded. He pulled back the curtain and peered out into the darkness. He saw nothing. No one was there and that was never a good sign.

Booker stood at the front door with his fingers curled around the doorknob.

"Open it," Wyatt commanded with his gun at the ready.

Standing to the side, Booker unlocked the door and opened it a few inches. He peered his head outside. "Clear."

"Fuck." Wyatt raced through the house with his heart in his throat. There was no back door, but there was a window.

Kirby and Callie sat on the edge of his bed, safe and sound. He let out a sigh of relief. "You girls okay?" He went right to the window and peeked through the curtain.

Booker stepped inside. "Gunn is here and he's doing a perimeter check. Xavier and Hunter are five minutes away."

"What the hell do you think that was about?" Kirby asked.

"I suspect it was Kofi wanting to know a little about me and how fast the cavalry would show." Wyatt rolled his shoulders. "Because no kid on this block would dare play ding dong ditch with me."

"So, what do we do now?" Kirby asked.

Wyatt glanced around the room. There was only one thing to do and he didn't like it. "We invite Kofi in."

"Excuse me?" Kirby jumped to her feet. "What the hell do you mean by that?"

"Not literally, but the only way to end this is to let him believe he can have the upper hand in our territory." Wyatt set his gun on the dresser.

"What are you thinking?" Booker asked.

Wyatt couldn't believe he entertained this idea, especially after the baby news, but it was the fastest, most effective way to draw Kofi out. "We let Kirby go see her wolves, seemingly alone tomorrow." He held Kirby's gaze. "You won't be, but we need to let him get close."

Kirby visibly shivered. "I want this nightmare to end."

Wyatt nodded. "It's not a good idea for us to stay here tonight. My couch in the office pulls into a sofa bed. We'll head there for the night and meet everyone at six sharp. I'll call Stone and let him know what happened."

"Why wait," Callie said. "There are photographers who come to take pictures of the wolves every morning at the ugly crack of dawn. We can use that."

"What do you mean?" Booker asked.

"They sit on that ridge with their binoculars, trying to catch a glimpse. We can put more men there along with a fake news story about Kirby." Callie glanced at her watch. "It's not ten yet. We've got the contacts. Why not have someone report that Kirby will be there at a specific time?"

"That will bring out everyone and their brother," Booker said.

"No, it won't." Wyatt pinched the bridge of his nose. "The photographers aren't there to see Kirby; they want an image of the wolves who generally only come out at dusk and dawn. The story will confirm where Kirby is doing her work, pinning down the location of her study, or at least where we want Kofi and his men to be. Doing it at dawn means there are a limited number of people in the area and less of the chance of collateral damage to humans and to wolves. I hate the idea and at the same time I can see the brilliance of it."

"Let me call my friends at the local news station." Callie waved her phone. "I'll need locations sooner rather than later. The clock is ticking."

"Let's get this show on the road." Wyatt knelt in front of Kirby, cupping her face. "Are you up for this?"

"Yes," she said. "Let's do it."

He brushed his lips across her mouth. There was more at stake here than protecting her and her wolves.

This was his family. His future. And he'd be damned if he was going to let anyone take it.

CHAPTER 16

Wyatt lifted his night vision goggles and scanned the ridge. It would be a good two hours before the sun crested over the hills. He tapped his earpiece. "Everyone in place?"

"I'm on the ridge with Gunn," Xavier said. "Two men with thick African accents present."

"One mile up the west hill," Booker's voice came over the comms. "I have my sights on the ridge as well as you and Kirby. Looking good."

"East side of the ridge covered," Hunter said. "One blind spot. Can't see Ridley, but I can see beyond him to Booker."

Wyatt scanned for Booker but couldn't find him, which made him nervous.

"I have movement north of the wolf den," Booker said. "Two men. Both are armed with AK-47s. I don't see Kofi anywhere, but I'd say Wyatt's about to be in sight."

Wyatt worried that no one had eyes on Ridley and that he hadn't responded to comms, but he'd have to let that go for now. "That's my cue to hide." He squeezed Kirby's shoulder. "Stay low. Just because you're wearing a bulletproof vest under this jacket doesn't mean they won't aim for your head."

"That doesn't help my anxiety any."

"I'll be ten paces behind," he said. "I've got your six." The sound of a gun being cocked echoed between his ears. He froze, blinking once. Fuck. Slowly, he glanced over his shoulder.

Kofi smiled from his position on the ground, his weapon aimed right for the back of Kirby's head. "You're a fool if you didn't think I saw this plan from a mile away," Kofi said in broken English and a thick accent. "Hand over your gun and anything else you might have on you. Don't make any rash or stupid decisions. My men will take out yours in a second, and I don't believe either of us wants that kind of bloodshed."

The only question in Wyatt's mind now was how Kofi managed to get so close without anyone knowing, and there was only one answer.

Ridley.

But why?

Not only had Callie made a few phone calls to her contacts inside the DEA, but so had the Brotherhood

Protectors. Ridley had checked out to be one of the good guys. He had a stellar record. No marks. Nothing in his background that would even suggest he was one of the bad guys. He'd fought side by side when the SEALs had been injured. Too many things pointed in a different direction. So, why would Ridley set them up? It didn't make sense.

Unless Kofi was holding something over his head.

"You're the fool in this situation." Wyatt stood tall and dropped his gun to the ground. "What are you going to do, shoot her right here with a group of photographers as witnesses?"

"For a smart man, you really are an idiot." Kofi shook his head. "Look around you. You're in the middle of the great outdoors. There are all sorts of animals out here that will kill you in an instant. All she has to do is get too close to an alpha gray wolf, his mate, and their cubs and she's breakfast."

"So, it's death by wolf mauling, is it?" Just as Wyatt and his team had predicted. The one thing that Kofi had neglected to do was ask Wyatt for his comms, which was still nestled in his ear and his entire team could hear his end of the conversation.

"Hold tight," Booker whispered. "There's a plan in play. It will make sense when you see it."

That didn't make him feel any better.

"Wolves don't attack unless provoked," Kirby added. "They will scatter before they come at me." She rose to her knees.

"Stay down," Wyatt commanded.

She flattened her stomach to the ground.

"Not if they see you as food." Kofi showed a large knife, holding it to his side. "Bloody, fresh meat. They will smell it and come running the second I slice you open."

Wyatt narrowed his eyes and growled. "Touch her with that blade and I will fucking kill you."

"No, you won't." Kofi lifted his fingers to his mouth and whistled. "The men you've been watching have been a decoy. The rest of my guys have been rounding up wolves all night. I've got them in cages over that hill. They're waiting to be released. They're angry and hungry. Neither of you stand a chance."

Out of the corner of Wyatt's eye, he noticed Ridley coming down from the hill behind Kofi. That motherfucker. "You asshole," he muttered. "You set me up."

Ridley shrugged. "It would appear that I did." He strolled in Wyatt's direction as if he didn't have a care in the world with his weapon at his side. "But I had my reasons and not everything is as it appears."

"Glad you could join the fun," Kofi said. "Having a DEA agent in my pocket is always nice."

"When did this alliance happen?" Wyatt needed to buy time until he saw this great plan that Booker had mentioned. Right about now would be a good time to explain it to him because he was getting damn sick and tired of talking.

"A funny thing about alliances, they shift." Ridley raised his gun in Wyatt's direction. "Or maybe they never do and it's all a game of cat and mouse to achieve one's end goal." Quickly, he widened his stance, aiming his weapon at Kofi. "Trusting a DEA agent who suddenly wants a piece of the action isn't the wisest move."

"What the fuck?" Kofi lunged.

Bang!

Ridley fired one round at Kofi's kneecap. "Money is not my language and you're the fool to believe it was."

Kofi screamed, dropping to the ground.

Wyatt lurched forward, yanking the knife from Kofi's hand while Ridley snagged the man's weapon. "Someone could have let me in on this new fucking plan."

"I couldn't. Not until everyone was in place and Kofi had crossed the ridge." Ridley pulled out a pair of handcuffs. "Besides, you would have never gone for it."

"Damn fucking right I wouldn't have. You put my fucking girlfriend and baby at risk."

"Baby?" Ridley asked.

"Baby?"

"Baby?"

"You're having a baby?"

He planted his hands on his hips and closed his eyes while his entire team kept repeating the question in his ear. "Shut the fuck up, everyone. I misspoke."

Laughter erupted.

"I guess we're not keeping that a secret anymore." Kirby took Ridley's hand and jumped to her feet, wiping the dirt from her jeans. "I take it everyone heard you over your comms."

"That they did," Wyatt whispered.

"Congratulations, ma'am." Ridley smiled. "I'm sorry I couldn't read you in and that I upset Wyatt. I didn't see any other way. I knew if Kofi thought he had someone on the inside, he'd be able to make this go away without bringing attention to himself and he could go back to the Congo and be back in business with a DEA agent in his pocket. It was a win-win in my book."

"You're uninvited to our wedding," Wyatt mumbled, blinking.

"Oh, and he proposed. Good man."

"He didn't and if he does, you'll be the first one I invite." Kirby kissed Ridley's cheek.

Kofi continued to moan and groan. "I need medical attention."

"An ambulance is on the way." Ridley pointed in the direction of the main road. "And a team of highly skilled professionals to deal with your sorry ass before they haul you off to jail in this country, where you'll spend some time in prison before going back to your own country where the penalty will be pretty stiff."

"You won't get away with this," Kofi yelled.

Wyatt took his comms out of his ear and stuffed it in his pocket. He wrapped his arms around Kirby. "I'm sorry I blasted our news out there for everyone."

"They were going to find out eventually." She palmed his cheek. "Is this really over?"

He glanced at Ridley, who nodded. "I believe so."

"I love you," she whispered.

"I love you, too." Wyatt had been on a million missions in his career but none as important as the mission he was about to embark on. Being a loving and caring father to his child and the kind of man his family could be proud of.

CHAPTER 17

WYATT STOOD in front of the grill outside the hangar and placed the last of the burgers and hot dogs on a platter.

"Did you see Sally's newscast?" Booker asked.

"I did." Wyatt nodded. "She did a great job reporting the story, and I have to say, I'm so fucking thrilled the ambassador finally got what he deserved."

"Ridley nailed his ass to the wall."

"I'm still pissed at you for not filling in me on that plan." Wyatt wasn't a grudge holder, but he'd harass Booker about it until the day he died.

"You would have done the same thing in my shoes, and don't try to tell me otherwise," Booker said. "Besides, like I've told you a million times, I didn't know until ten minutes before I switched positions. It happened that fast. We both know it was the best course of action."

"I will hold it over your head for a long while."

Booker laughed. "If you do, I'll have someone else be my best man."

"You wouldn't dare."

"How's Kirby feeling these days?" Booker asked.

"Not great," Wyatt admitted. "Throws up every goddamned morning and blames me for it."

"You did knock her up."

Wyatt rolled his eyes. "It takes two to make a baby, or didn't you learn that in biology."

"I still can't believe you're the first one of us to be a dad."

"Me either," Wyatt admitted. He took the tray and brought it to the table. Glancing around, he smiled. He had everything he could have ever dreamed of and more right here in Yellowstone.

Team Eagle. His brothers. His chosen family.

His forever home.

Never in a million years did he ever think he'd plant roots. It was one of the reasons he loved the Navy. Moving from place to place had always been part of the allure. He had a restless soul until Kirby captured his heart.

"But I'm looking forward to having a little boy or girl," he said.

"Are you going to find out?"

"Kirby doesn't want to and I'm fine with that. As long as he or she is healthy, I couldn't care less, but I think Kirby secretly hopes for a boy," Wyatt said. "How goes the wedding plans?"

"Venue is booked. Dress has been ordered. Not much is left to do but wait for the date to arrive." Booker and Callie were set to be married in two months. It was a bigger event than originally planned, but everyone at the Brotherhood Protectors was beyond excited for the happy couple.

Hunter and Layla were also expecting a child and couldn't be happier. So happy it was disgusting to watch, but it warmed Wyatt's heart to see Hunter with a woman who understood him in ways no one else could.

Gunn had found the perfect woman. One who matched his personality and kept him in check at every turn. They complimented each other and Wyatt suspected they too would soon be doing the waltz down the aisle.

And then there was Xavier and Allegra. What a pair. They had moved in together and were inseparable.

Everyone on his team had found the person who made their souls sing and home in Yellowstone.

"Hey there, handsome." Kirby placed her hand on his shoulder. "You have that weird look in your eye, like you're about to get all mushy on me."

He wrapped his arm around the love of his life. It was strange to feel that about a person after so many years of believing the only thing that mattered was his career. "I just might." He laughed. "What do you think of the new guys?"

"I'd met Knox Preston and Walker Pierce a few years ago," she said. "They're cool but seem a little out of sorts, like they're struggling to settle in."

"Not sure they've come to terms with leaving the military or what the Brotherhood is all about yet, but once they land their first assignment, it will all fall into place. They're ready, so it's just a matter of time."

"Colton Henderson's an interesting character. I like him, but Corbin River seems a little lost. He's quiet and he's so young."

"He's not thirty yet," Wyatt said. "And he's very lost. But he'll get his footing. He's got us to lean on." He kissed his fiancée's cheek. He wasn't sure life could get any better than this. "I'm sorry I couldn't make it to the doctor's appointment today. I'll make it up to you when you go to that ultrasound thingy next month."

"Oh, they had to do that today."

He jerked his head back. "Why? Is something wrong?"

"That depends on if you think twins will be a problem for you?" She smiled.

"Did you just say twins? As in two babies?" He stumbled backward, landing his ass on the picnic table bench.

"Are you okay?" She sat next to him, squeezing his thigh.

He palmed her cheek. "I'm better than okay, but what about you? Doesn't that make the pregnancy harder?"

"It means we're only doing this once." She laughed. "Daddy."

"I've never been so happy and I love you." He brushed his lips over her mouth. "Mommy."

Team EAGLE
Booker's Mission - Kris Norris
Hunter's Mission - Kendall Talbot
Gunn's Mission - Delilah Devlin
Xavier's Mission - Lori Matthews
Wyatt's Mission - Jen Talty

Thanks for taking the time to read *Wyatt's Mission*.
Please feel free to leave an honest review!
If you'd like to learn more about Corbin River, please check out his parents story in **Kisses Sweeter than Wine.**

Grab a glass of vino, kick back, relax, and let the romance roll in…
Sign up for my [Newsletter (https://dl.bookfunnel.com/82gm8b9k4y)](https://dl.bookfunnel.com/82gm8b9k4y) where I often give away free books before publication.

Join my private [Facebook group](https://www.facebook.com/groups/191706547909047/) where I post exclusive excerpts and discuss all things murder and love!

ALSO BY JEN TALTY

Brand new series: SAFE HARBOR!

Mine To Keep

Mine To Save

Mine To Protect

Mine to Hold

Mine to Love

Check out LOVE IN THE ADIRONDACKS!

Shattered Dreams

An Inconvenient Flame

The Wedding Driver

Clear Blue Sky

Blue Moon

Before the Storm

NY STATE TROOPER SERIES (also set in the Adirondacks!)

In Two Weeks

Dark Water

Deadly Secrets

Murder in Paradise Bay

To Protect His own

Deadly Seduction

When A Stranger Calls

His Deadly Past

The Corkscrew Killer

First Responders: A spin-off from the NY State Troopers series

Playing With Fire

Private Conversation

The Right Groom

After The Fire

Caught In The Flames

Chasing The Fire

Legacy Series

Dark Legacy

Legacy of Lies

Secret Legacy

Emerald City

Investigate Away

Sail Away

Fly Away

Flirt Away

Colorado Brotherhood Protectors

Fighting For Esme

Defending Raven

Fay's Six

Darius' Promise

Yellowstone Brotherhood Protectors

Guarding Payton

Candlewood Falls

Rivers Edge

The Buried Secret

Its In His Kiss

Lips Of An Angel

Kisses Sweeter than Wine

A Little Bit Whiskey

It's all in the Whiskey

Johnnie Walker

Georgia Moon

Jack Daniels

Jim Beam

Whiskey Sour

Whiskey Cobbler

Whiskey Smash

Irish Whiskey

The Monroes

Color Me Yours

Color Me Smart

Color Me Free

Color Me Lucky

Color Me Ice

Color Me Home

Search and Rescue

Protecting Ainsley

Protecting Clover

Protecting Olympia

Protecting Freedom

Protecting Princess

Protecting Marlowe

Fallport Rescue Operations

Searching for Madison

DELTA FORCE-NEXT GENERATION

Shielding Jolene

Shielding Aalyiah

Shielding Laine

Shielding Talullah

Shielding Maribel

Shielding Daisy

The Men of Thief Lake
Rekindled
Destiny's Dream

Federal Investigators
Jane Doe's Return
The Butterfly Murders

THE AEGIS NETWORK
The Sarich Brother
The Lighthouse
Her Last Hope
The Last Flight
The Return Home
The Matriarch

Aegis Network: Jacksonville Division
A SEAL's Honor

Aegis Network Short Stories
Max & Milian
A Christmas Miracle
Spinning Wheels
Holiday's Vacation

Special Forces Operation Alpha

Burning Desire

Burning Kiss

Burning Skies

Burning Lies

Burning Heart

Burning Bed

Remember Me Always

The Brotherhood Protectors

Out of the Wild

Rough Justice

Rough Around The Edges

Rough Ride

Rough Edge

Rough Beauty

The Brotherhood Protectors

The Saving Series

Saving Love

Saving Magnolia

Saving Leather

Hot Hunks

Cove's Blind Date Blows Up

My Everyday Hero – Ledger

Tempting Tavor

Malachi's Mystic Assignment

Needing Neor

Holiday Romances

A Christmas Getaway

Alaskan Christmas

Whispers

Christmas In The Sand

Heroes & Heroines on the Field

Taking A Risk

Tee Time

A New Dawn

The Blind Date

Spring Fling

Summers Gone

Winter Wedding

The Awakening

The Collective Order

The Lost Sister

The Lost Soldier

The Lost Soul

The Lost Connection

The New Order

ABOUT JEN TALTY

Jen Talty is the *USA Today* Bestselling Author of Contemporary Romance, Romantic Suspense, and Paranormal Romance. In the fall of 2020, her short story was selected and featured in a 1001 Dark Nights Anthology.

Regardless of the genre, her goal is to take you on a ride that will leave you floating under the sun with warmth in your heart. She writes stories about broken heroes and heroines who aren't necessarily looking for romance, but in the end, they find the kind of love books are written about :).

She first started writing while carting her kids to one hockey rink after the other, averaging 170 games per year between 3 kids in 2 countries and 5 states. Her first book, IN TWO WEEKS was originally published in 2007. In 2010 she helped form a publishing company (Cool Gus Publishing) with *NY Times* Bestselling Author Bob Mayer where she ran the technical side of the business through 2016.

Jen is currently enjoying the next phase of her life... the empty nester! She and her husband reside in Jupiter, Florida.

Grab a glass of vino, kick back, relax, and let the romance roll in...

Sign up for my [Newsletter (https://dl.bookfunnel.com/82gm8b9k4y)](https://dl.bookfunnel.com/82gm8b9k4y) where I often give away free books before publication.

Join my private [Facebook group](https://www.facebook.com/groups/191706547909047/) (https://www.facebook.com/groups/191706547909047/) where I post exclusive excerpts and discuss all things murder and love!

Never miss a new release. Follow me on Amazon:amazon.com/author/jentalty

And on Bookbub: bookbub.com/authors/jen-talty

BROTHERHOOD PROTECTORS
ORIGINAL SERIES BY ELLE JAMES

Bayou Brotherhood Protectors

Remy (#1)

Gerard (#2)

Lucas (#3)

Beau (#4)

Rafael (#5)

Valentin (#6)

Landry (#7)

Simon (#8)

Maurice (#9)

Jacques (#10)

Brotherhood Protectors Yellowstone

Saving Kyla (#1)

Saving Chelsea (#2)

Saving Amanda (#3)

Saving Liliana (#4)

Saving Breely (#5)

Saving Savvie (#6)

Saving Jenna (#7)

Saving Peyton (#8)

Brotherhood Protectors Colorado

SEAL Salvation (#1)

Rocky Mountain Rescue (#2)

Ranger Redemption (#3)

Tactical Takeover (#4)

Colorado Conspiracy (#5)

Rocky Mountain Madness (#6)

Free Fall (#7)

Colorado Cold Case (#8)

Fool's Folly (#9)

Colorado Free Rein (#10)

Rocky Mountain Venom (#11)

High Country Hero (#12)

Brotherhood Protectors

Montana SEAL (#1)

Bride Protector SEAL (#2)

Montana D-Force (#3)

Cowboy D-Force (#4)

Montana Ranger (#5)

Montana Dog Soldier (#6)

Montana SEAL Daddy (#7)

Montana Ranger's Wedding Vow (#8)

Montana SEAL Undercover Daddy (#9)

Cape Cod SEAL Rescue (#10)

Montana SEAL Friendly Fire (#11)

Montana SEAL's Mail-Order Bride (#12)

SEAL Justice (#13)

Ranger Creed (#14)

Delta Force Rescue (#15)

Dog Days of Christmas (#16)

Montana Rescue (#17)

Montana Ranger Returns (#18)

Hot SEAL Salty Dog (SEALs in Paradise)

Hot SEAL, Hawaiian Nights (SEALs in Paradise)

Hot SEAL Bachelor Party (SEALs in Paradise)

Hot SEAL, Independence Day (SEALs in Paradise)

Brotherhood Protectors Boxed Set 1

Brotherhood Protectors Boxed Set 2

Brotherhood Protectors Boxed Set 3

Brotherhood Protectors Boxed Set 4

Brotherhood Protectors Boxed Set 5

Brotherhood Protectors Boxed Set 6

ABOUT ELLE JAMES

ELLE JAMES also writing as MYLA JACKSON is a *New York Times* and *USA Today* Bestselling author of books including cowboys, intrigues and paranormal adventures that keep her readers on the edges of their seats. When she's not at her computer, she's traveling, snow skiing, boating, or riding her ATV, dreaming up new stories. Learn more about Elle James at www.ellejames.com

Website | Facebook | Twitter | GoodReads | Newsletter | BookBub | Amazon

Or visit her alter ego Myla Jackson at
mylajackson.com
Website | Facebook | Twitter | Newsletter

Follow Me!
www.ellejames.com
ellejamesauthor@gmail.com

Manufactured by Amazon.ca
Bolton, ON